MW01126767

Frayed Edges

A MARY O'REILLY PARANORMAL MYSTERY

(Book Seventeen)

by

Terri Reid

FRAYED EDGES – A MARY O'REILLY
PARANORMAL MYSTERY

by

Terri Reid

The author would like to thank all those who have contributed to the creation of this book: Richard Reid, Sarah Powers and Hillary Gadd. Also, thank you to Jennifer Bates, John and Vicki Daley, and Virginia Onines for the time they took to beta read this book.

She would also like to thank all of the wonderful readers who walk with her through Mary and Bradley's adventures and encourage her along the way. I hope we continue on this wonderful journey for a long time.

Prologue

The super moon loomed over the harvested cornfield, its bright yellow glow illuminating the rows of stubbled plants and occasional missed ear of corn. Those forgotten ears of corn were exactly the prize honor student Ruth McCredie was pursuing. Parking her late-model car in the parking lot of the Convention and Visitors Bureau across from the field, Ruth then made her way across the country road, jogging slightly to the north to avoid being seen by passing vehicles on busy Highway 20. She didn't think what she was doing was illegal, but she didn't want to have to explain why she was walking through a cornfield at nearly midnight.

Standing on the edge of the ditch separating the road from the field, Ruth looked around. The moonlight was so bright that she stuck her flashlight into her backpack with a shrug and started across the ditch without it. The ditch was steep and she nearly lost her footing as she climbed up on the field side, but digging her hiking boots into the soft dirt, she was able to catch herself and reach the other side.

Stopping at the edge of the field, she looked down at the ground, scanning it quickly. She knew the outside perimeter of the field was the most vulnerable spot, so she needed to grab samples from this area quickly and move on toward the center of the field. She finally spotted a nearly complete ear of corn, its browned husk curling at the edges. She knelt down, picked it up and separated the protective leaves and fine strands of silk. The corn inside looked perfect, untouched by raccoons and insects. Pulling a plastic bag from an outside pocket of her backpack, she placed the ear inside the bag, sealed it and wrote on the outside with a black marker. "October 27, 2015. Exterior row. Southeast quadrant. Near Gund Cemetery."

Sliding the filled bag into her backpack, she sighed with satisfaction. This was going to work. The samples from this final field would be enough to prove her theory. She was bound to ace this class and, if she was lucky, qualify for the scholarship.

Zipping her backpack up, she stood and moved across the field, stepping over the rows rather than walking down them to get to the center of the field. The crop had been recently harvested, so depending on whether the tractor wheels had rolled down the row, the ground below her varied from very soft dirt to hard, compacted soil. She walked carefully, looking down at the ground, not knowing what kind of footing to expect, and not wanting to fall and cut her hands on the sharply spiked harvest remnants.

Hearing movement ahead of her, she froze, her heart thumping in her chest. She looked up and released a sigh of relief as she watched a small herd of white-tailed deer run swiftly along the edge of the field that bordered the Gund Cemetery. She watched them leap gracefully across the rows that she had been struggling to cross. "Show-offs," she chuckled softly, then shook her head with resignation and continued her trek. A similar noise ahead of her did not distract her this time from her progress. The super moon was probably confusing the deer population from knowing whether it was daytime or night, she decided.

"I wonder if there have been any studies researching deer movement during the full moon," she mused softly as she stepped over an unusually high row.

Stopping, she looked around, getting her bearings. She was about in the middle of the field, she decided. This would be a good place to get a few more samples. She looked back at the row she was standing in and saw four ears laying in the dirt.

"Perfect," she said, reaching back for another plastic bag. "These will be great."

Hurrying down the row towards the ears, she was surprised to hear a crack in the distance. Before she could react, she felt the blow of the bullet entering her body. She stared, wide-eyed, at the blood blossoming across her sweatshirt.

"I've been..." she began, more bewildered than afraid, but then her knees gave out and she fell to the ground. The soft earth absorbed the impact from the fall, but a sharp stalk scraped her face. She gasped in pain, but the gasp gave way to choking as her life ebbed away, the rich, brown soil absorbing her blood.

Chapter One

"Corn pudding?" Bradley called from the bathroom, his voice a mixture of horror and disgust. "Who in their right mind puts corn in pudding?"

Mary leaned against the doorjamb, enjoying the sight of her husband dressed only in a towel while he leaned over the sink, peering into the mirror as he shaved. The smells that were carried in the bathroom's steam were uniquely male, cedar, musk and a slight hint of mint.

She inhaled deeply and sighed her approval. Bradley turned sharply to look at her. "Are you okay?" he asked, concern furrowing the lines between his eyes.

She smiled and nodded. "Yes, I'm fine," she said. "I was just enjoying the moment."

He shook his head, mystified. "What moment?"

She mentally rolled her eyes. "The moment of standing here, watching my incredibly sexy husband with only a towel draped around his waist shave his face," she said. "It's a very sensual experience, from the scent of male in the air, to the sound of your razor against your face."

Grinning, he picked up a hand towel and wiped off the excess shaving cream. "You think I'm sexy?" he asked.

Chuckling, she walked towards him, fingering the edge of the tucked in towel. "I know how you could be even sexier," she whispered up to him.

Passion filled his eyes for a moment, and then it was replaced with remorse. "I can't," he said. "I've got an eight o'clock meeting with the mayor. I can't miss it."

She sighed, but this time it was filled with regret. "I know," she agreed. "I've got places to go, too. It was just…"

He bent down and kissed her slowly and deeply. "A really good idea," he finished for her as he lifted his head. "And one that I promise to take you up on this evening."

"Promise?" she teased.

"More than promise," he replied.

He moved past her into the bedroom, opened his dresser and pulled his underclothes out. "So, what do you have planned for today?" he asked. "You're not dressed for the office."

She looked down at her maternity flannel shirt and jeans and nodded. "I'm going out to Gund Cemetery again," she replied.

6

He stopped halfway through pulling a t-shirt over his head and looked at her. "Okay, remind me again, Gund Cemetery?"

Sitting on the edge of their bed, she nodded. "It's out near the Visitors Center," she said. "And it's still an active cemetery. But in the late 1800s a town a little north of the cemetery got hit with the cholera epidemic. It was so bad, so many people died, that all the few survivors could manage was a mass grave instead of individual ones. The survivors planted an oak tree in remembrance of the dead, hoping it would be enough to help them pass over. But, whether it was because of the suddenness of their deaths or the lack of a proper burial, many of the spirits are still hanging around."

He shrugged into his shirt. "You've been out there a number of times," he said. "Don't they want to cross over?"

Mary nodded. "Yes, they do," she explained. "But they've been dead for over a hundred years, so some of them are pretty shy about letting me approach them. The children were easy, most of them have crossed over now. It's the adults that are the hardest."

Bradley shook his head. "You constantly amaze me," he said with an admiring smile. "How many people would stand in a cemetery in the middle of November to help dead people cross over?"

She laughed. "Um, not too many," she agreed. "Most people probably wouldn't even think it was a thing to do."

He shrugged. "Well, okay, that's true," he agreed, coming over to stand next to the bed. "But you, my darling wife, are amazing."

She smiled up at him. "And you trust me?" she asked.

"Completely," he replied, lowering his face towards hers.

"Good, so I can put corn pudding on the Thanksgiving menu?" she inserted, just before their lips touched.

He pulled back and stared down at her. "That was tricky," he said.

"Uh-huh," she grinned back.

He rolled his eyes. "Fine," he said. "I'll try it. But I don't think I'm going to like it."

She reached up and wrapped her arms around his neck. "Oh, believe me," she said, pulling him down towards her. "You're going to love it."

After the kiss, Bradley slipped his arms to her waist and held her while he looked into her eyes. "All kidding aside," he said seriously, "are you sure you should be taking on Thanksgiving and a surprise birthday party for Clarissa?"

"I'm fine," she insisted. "I have two more months to go, and I feel really healthy and strong. Besides, this is Clarissa's first birthday with us, and it needs to be special."

"It doesn't need to be an extravaganza," he argued. "We could just have ice cream, cake and a few presents."

Mary shook her head. "We need to make up for all those parties we missed," she said. "Besides, we need to give her a little extra attention before Mikey is born. I really want to do this."

Sighing softly, he pulled her into his arms and kissed her gently. "You will promise me that you'll ask for help if you need it?" he demanded softly.

"Yes," she agreed. "I promise I'll call in the troops if I feel overwhelmed."

"Thank you," he said. "But don't wait until you're overwhelmed, and don't go crazy. You're her mother, not her fairy godmother."

"Her mother," Mary repeated softly, her eyes widening in shock. "Crap."

"What's wrong?" Bradley asked.

Shaking her head, Mary stepped away from him. "Nothing," she insisted. "Nothing at all. I just remembered a promise I made."

"That's it?" he asked, eyeing her suspiciously.

"Yes," she said with a wide and, she hoped, innocent smile. "That's it."

She waited until Bradley went downstairs before she rushed across the room and tossed open the closet door. First she lumbered down to her hands and knees to search behind the shoes and boxes on the floor. Then she pushed the hung clothing to the side to see if there was anything caught behind them. Finally, she pulled a chair over and climbed up to search the shelves. She pushed shoeboxes and plastic storage cases to the side, searching desperately when she finally saw the white, crumpled shopping bag from a chain fabric store. "There it is," she muttered as she reached as far as she could to catch hold of the corner of the bag.

Pulling it out, she slowly climbed down from the chair and then sat on it, pulling out the partially finished pink quilt. "Sorry, Jeannine," she whispered. "I nearly forgot I promised to finish this for her. I'll get it done for her birthday."

Carefully folding it and placing it back in the bag, she laid it on her bed. "I can do it," she said to herself. "How hard can quilting be?"

Chapter Two

"Do I really have to go to school today?" Clarissa asked as she sat at the kitchen table eating her breakfast. Lucky, her black kitten, sat beside her on her chair, batting at a ribbon in Clarissa's hair.

"Of course you do," Bradley replied. "Why would you want to stay home?"

Turning in her chair to face her father, she shook her head in excitement. "Because it's almost Thanksgiving and Grandma and Grandpa O'Reilly are coming to stay with us and there's so much to do!"

Chuckling, Bradley shook his head. "Well, it's only Monday, so we have a few more days to wait until Thanksgiving," he said. "And Grandma and Grandpa won't be coming until Wednesday. So, why don't you try to concentrate on school for at least a couple more days, okay?"

Picking up a spoonful of oatmeal, Clarissa sighed. "Fine, I guess."

"Fine, I guess," Bradley mimicked, making sure his voice was sadder and more pathetic than Clarissa's. "I hope you survive."

Trying to hide a giggle, Clarissa shook her head. "Everything in this world takes so long."

11

"Tell me about it," Mary said, sitting down next to them at the table. She winked at Clarissa. "Can you remind me how long I've been pregnant?"

Shrugging her shoulders and with a twinkle in her eyes, Clarissa turned to her mother and replied, "At least three years. Or maybe even longer."

Mary nodded. "Exactly what I thought, too," she replied, placing her hands on her belly. "Hey, Mikey, it's time for you to move out of there and get a life."

Laughing, Clarissa leaned over so she was close to Mary's belly. "Hey, Mikey, if you come before Christmas, Santa will bring you stuff."

They were all delighted when Mikey moved inside Mary, causing her belly to shift sideways. "Well," Mary said with a laugh. "Looks like he's packing his bags."

She looked over at Clarissa. "So, what's in the plans for school this week?" she asked.

"We are learning about the pilgrims," Clarissa said. "And about the first Thanksgiving."

"That's cool," Bradley replied. "Make sure you ask your teacher if they served corn pudding for dinner."

"Bradley," Mary said, lightly slapping his arm. "That's not nice."

Chuckling, he stood up, gave both Mary and Clarissa a kiss and then slipped on his coat. "Okay, no more corn pudding jokes," he said. "But can we at least have pumpkin pie for dessert?"

"With whipping cream," Clarissa added.

"Well, of course," Mary said. "And apple pie, and cherry pie, and probably something even more delicious because Rosie is bringing a dessert."

Bradley paused and looked down at his waistline. "Yeah, maybe I'll jog to work this week," he said.

"The weatherman said it's supposed to snow today," Clarissa said, picking up her bowl and carrying it to the sink. "So you probably should drive your chief car."

Mary grinned at Clarissa's nickname for Bradley's cruiser. "And, in case of emergency," Mary added. "It's so much more professional when the police chief isn't running down the street making his own siren sounds."

"Good point," Bradley replied with a smile. "Maybe I'll just have to spend more time working out." He glanced over at his wife. "That's right. We were going to work out this evening, weren't we?"

She blushed slightly and nodded. "Yes. Yes, we were," she said. "So don't work too late."

"I won't," he said. "Call me when you get home from the cemetery."

"I will," Mary replied.

Once the door closed, Clarissa hurried to the closet and pulled out her coat. "Can Maggie come over for Thanksgiving?" she asked.

"Isn't Maggie having Thanksgiving with her family?" Mary asked.

Slipping on her coat, Clarissa nodded. "Yeah, but she said her Thanksgiving is boring compared to our Thanksgiving," she said. "She just has her plain, old family, and we have lots of people."

"Well, I'll call the Brennans and see if they want to join us for Thanksgiving," Mary said. "How about that?"

"That would be so cool," Clarissa replied as she picked up her backpack.

Mary came over and gave Clarissa and hug and a kiss. "Have an excellent day at school today," she said.

"Thanks," Clarissa replied. "And you have an excellent day at the cemetery."

Mary laughed. "Thank you. I will."

Chapter Three

Snow was falling, a light dusting that turned the empty farmers' fields into a winter wonderland. Mary turned off Highway 20 onto Brown's Mill Road. She drove past the entrance to the Stephenson County Convention and Visitors Bureau building, with a parking lot filled with people traveling to Galena to get an early start on the Thanksgiving holiday, and continued a little farther up the road.

The new SUV they bought several weeks ago was four-wheel drive and handled well on the narrow, gravel road that surrounded the cemetery. She pulled past the stone marker and drove a few more yards ahead, leaving enough room for another vehicle to pull in behind her, just in case there was a visitor to the cemetery. Placing the car in park, she turned off the engine and slipped her gloves on before she climbed out of the vehicle.

The stone marker next to the drive had "Gund Cemetery, Established 1850" carved into its face. Mary glanced back at the marker and the ornate, wrought iron archway that welcomed visitors to the long and narrow strip of hallowed ground. The cemetery was less than 100 yards wide, but nearly 500 yards long. And of course, Mary thought with resignation, the area she needed to reach was at the far end. Typical of rural cemeteries, there were fields surrounding it on three sides, and on this cold, snowy morning, there was nothing to stop the sharp wind that stung Mary's face.

She took a deep breath, forced herself to clear her thoughts and slowly gazed around, allowing her unique ability to come to the forefront. Slowly, images of people dressed in old-fashioned clothing appeared at the far end of the cemetery, gazing at her in curiosity. She smiled at them and nodded, then casually walked towards them.

"Good morning," she said, her voice appearing as puffs of steam as she spoke. "It's a lovely day."

The ghosts were dressed in summer clothing and were not affected by the cold or the snow. Their deaths occurred in the summer, and their spirits were confined to that season. During Mary's first visit, several small children had stopped chasing each other and hurried over to talk to her, the friendly stranger in their cemetery. They were open and trusting, and she had no problem teaching them how to look for and walk into the light. But now, most of the children were gone, and she was working with the adults. It was a slow process, but she felt that she was beginning to gain their trust.

She finally made it to the oak tree at the far end of the cemetery, its leaves brown and leathery, still attached to the branches. The old oak had been planted as a seedling over the mass grave of the

16

cholera victims over 100 years ago, and now, its ancient branches spread wide and tall, protecting the hallowed ground.

Mary gazed around at the spirits watching her and decided on her next challenge. There was one group of women who had avoided her and huddled together near the fence line. They would look in her direction and speak to each other, but none ever attempted to speak with her.

"Old-fashioned mean girls?" Mary murmured to herself. "Well, this isn't high school, and I'm not going to be put off by them."

She purposely walked in their direction, meeting their eyes and nodding as she got close. "Good morning," Mary said directly to one of the women she'd seen before.

She was surprised when the woman came over to meet her. "I need to show you something," the woman said, motioning urgently.

Mary followed, interested to see what the woman wanted to show her. They walked to the edge of the cemetery, and the woman pointed out into the distance. "Do you see her?" she asked, her arm raised. "There in the field?"

Mary squinted her eyes, and sure enough, the air seemed to vibrate and then solidify. She could see the spirit of a young woman standing in the field, looking around. The spirit glided around the area, as if she was searching for something, and then turned and looked the other way.

"She's not one of us," the spirit standing next to Mary said. "She's only been out there for a little while. And I think she's lost."

Mary studied the ghost. The young woman was dressed in jeans and a sweatshirt with the logo of the local university, definitely not one of the spirits from the 1800s.

Looking up and down the fence, Mary sighed, deciding it was too high for her to climb over in her current condition. She was going to have to walk all the way back to the road. The ghost next to her smiled with understanding. "There is a break in the fence a short walk to the west. I can show you," she offered.

Mary nodded gratefully. "Thank you," she said. "I would really appreciate it."

The break was just large enough for Mary to slide through and walk onto the field. She carefully navigated the rows and ends of dried corn stalks sticking out of the ground, not wanting to stumble on the frozen ground. She stopped when she was several rows away from where the spirit lingered, and slowly scanned the area. If this was a crime scene, she certainly did not want to get any closer and risk contaminating the area.

The new covering of snow made it difficult to discern objects underneath the white blanket, and she couldn't tell if the lumps she saw between the rows were a body or upturned clumps of soil. "Hello," she called out to the spirit.

The spirit stopped her movement and turned to Mary. "You can see me?" she asked.

Mary nodded. "Yes, I can," she said. "And I'd like to help you."

The ghost glided closer, and Mary could see the stain of blood on the front of her sweatshirt, the soil entangled in her hair and the bright scratch on her face.

"I think…" the ghost paused for a moment and looked across the field again. "I think I might have been shot."

Mary nodded and met the ghost's eyes. "Do you remember when it happened?" Mary asked.

The ghost stood quietly for a moment, thinking about her answer. Then she looked up at Mary. "Am I dead?" she asked hesitantly, her voice a mere whisper.

"Yes," Mary replied gently. "Yes. I'm afraid you are."

A sad shudder passed through the ghost's frame. A translucent tear trailed down her cheek, and she looked away from Mary. "Well, that make sense," she said, her voice catching.

"Do you remember where it happened?" Mary asked.

The ghost turned and pointed to a row that was higher than most. Mary stepped onto the row in front of her, to give herself a little elevation and could see the shape of a body under the snow. Regret filled her heart, and tears filled her eyes. With remorse in her eyes, Mary turned back to the ghost of the young woman.

"I can see you," Mary said softly. "I can see where you fell."

"That's me?" the ghost asked, looking at the lifeless shape on the ground. "That's me?"

"I'm sorry," Mary said. "But, yes, I think it's you."

"How…how could this happen?" the young woman asked, looking down at the ground and slowly shaking her head. She turned back to look at Mary. "How?"

"I'm going to call the police," she said, "so, we can find out what happened to you."

The ghost nodded silently and returned to staring at her remains.

Pulling her cell phone out of her purse, Mary dialed Bradley's number. "Hi, it's me," she said when he answered. "You need to come out and meet me at Gund Cemetery. I have a feeling I may have just stumbled upon a homicide victim."

Chapter Four

Mary placed her cell phone back in her pocket and turned back to the ghost still staring silently at the ground. "I'm so sorry," Mary said.

The ghost turned back and shook her head. "I'm only twenty years old," she said, her voice breaking. "I had my whole life in front of me. Why would someone do this?"

"That's a very good question," Mary replied calmly. "And we are going to find that out. But first I need to know your name."

"Oh. Of course," the ghost replied, taking a deep breath. "My name is Ruth. Ruth McCredie."

"Hi, Ruth," Mary said. "I'm Mary. Mary O'Reilly Alden."

Ruth nodded. "Hi," she said, her voice still shaky. "So, what happens next?"

"Well, we wait until the police chief shows up and he asks you a bunch of questions," Mary said. "And then we figure out what happened."

Ruth looked around the field. "Do I have to stay here?" she asked. "Do I have to stay here in the field all by myself?"

"No," Mary said, shaking her head. "Now that you and I have met, you're going to be able to leave the field. And anytime you need me, all you have to do is think of me and you'll be where I am."

"That's weird," Ruth said, looking a little concerned.

"I know," Mary replied with a shrug and a sad smile. "But that's how it happens."

"Do you do this kind of thing all the time?" Ruth asked, her concern turning into intrigue. "Find dead people?"

Mary nodded. "Yeah, a lot," she said. "It's kind of what I do."

"Wow. I was studying agriculture in school," Ruth replied. "I didn't even know this was a thing."

Mary smiled. "Well, I don't know if it really is a thing," she said. "It's more like a natural talent. Or, I guess I should say supernatural talent."

Ruth chuckled sadly. "Good one."

Mary heard car tires on gravel and looked over to see Bradley's cruiser pull up and Bradley get out of the car. She was surprised when the door on the other side of the car opened and Alex Boettcher, the Stephenson County D.A., got out and joined Bradley as they walked across the field.

Bradley was dressed in his uniform, his jacket zipped and his work shoes easily covering the ground. Alex, as usual, was dressed like he had just walked off the pages of GQ magazine, with a three-piece suit and an open, black, cashmere overcoat flapping in the wind. Unfortunately, his leather dress shoes weren't quite as rugged as Bradley's shoes, so his pace was more measured so he didn't slip. Bradley easily outpaced him as they hurried towards her.

"Stop right there," Mary called to Bradley as he neared the area Ruth's body lay.

He froze in his tracks. "Where is the body?"

"One row ahead of you and about three yards to the east," Mary replied.

Bradley looked over and nodded. "I see it," he said.

"Her," Mary called back to him. "You see her."

Understanding dawned on his face and he nodded. "Thank you," he said. "I see her."

Alex reached Bradley and looked over. "Is that the body?" he asked.

"Yes, that's her," Bradley replied.

"And you know it's a female because…" Alex began. Then he stopped, looked over at Mary and shook his head. "I don't want to know, do I?"

"Her name is Ruth McCredie," Mary said. "She's twenty years old, and she was shot."

The men approached her body carefully, Alex following carefully in Bradley's footsteps. Kneeling next to her, Bradley gently brushed the snow from Ruth's face.

"That's really me," Ruth said, her voice hitching.

Bradley stood and pulled out his radio to call for an ambulance. Alex moved around him so he could see her face and then he sighed. "She's only a kid," he said. "I'm sure her parents are looking for her."

"My parents," Ruth gasped. "They must be worried sick."

"We'll contact them," Mary said. "We'll make sure someone goes to your house and talks to them."

Alex stood up, brushed the snow from his coat and turned to Mary. "Do you know when this happened?" he asked.

Mary turned to Ruth for the answer. "I was out here on the night of the super moon," Ruth explained. "Um, October 28th. I was picking up samples for a research project."

"The night of October 28th," Mary replied.

Slipping his radio back in his pocket, Bradley slowly scanned the area. "Were there any deer in the area that night?" he asked. "Could she have been mistakenly shot by a poacher?"

Ruth nodded. "There was a herd of deer that ran from the west side of the field towards the road just a few minutes before I was shot," she explained. "But it was pretty bright outside."

"There was a herd of deer in the area just before she was shot," Mary relayed. "But they had already run past her and were headed towards the road a few minutes before she was shot."

Alex stared at Mary for a moment, shook his head and then sighed. "Could you ask her if there was any reason someone would want to kill her?" he said with resignation in his voice.

Ruth shook her head sadly. "No, no reason," she said, her voice filled with emotion. "But that doesn't matter does it? Because now I'm dead."

Slipping her arms around her chest, Ruth hugged herself and sobbed softly. "I'm dead." Then she slowly faded away.

Chapter Five

"Mary… Mary," Alex called.

She had been so focused on Ruth's sorrow, Mary hadn't heard Alex calling to her. Turning, she shook her head to clear it. "I'm sorry," she replied. "What did you need?"

"Could you ask her —," he began.

"I'm sorry," Mary interrupted. "She's gone."

"Can you get her back?" Alex asked.

"No, it doesn't work like that," she said. "But I'm sure she'll contact me again. She…" Mary's voice caught in her throat. Suddenly it was just too much. This wasn't just another ghost she had to help move on from years ago. This was a young woman with her whole life in front of her. A young woman whose life someone else had decided wasn't worth anything. Tears burned her eyes, and she shook her head. She was so young. Why? Why would someone? How could someone?

She drew in a shuddering breath and tried to stem the tide of tears, but she knew it was too late. Turning away from the men, she reached into her pocket for a tissue to blot the tears on her face.

"Mary?" Bradley asked softly.

Still facing away, she waved her hand in an effort to ward him off. "Give me a minute," she called, trying to keep the sorrow out of her voice.

But, instead of waiting, he hurried over to her and gently pulled her into his arms. She felt Bradley's hands on her upper arms, and he gently turned her to face him.

"Please, I don't want…" she stammered, looking over at Alex and then back at Bradley.

Glancing over his shoulder, Bradley realized her dilemma and moved so his body blocked her from Alex's view. Lifting his hand, he tenderly wiped the tears from her cheeks. "This one's hard," he said softly.

She nodded and sniffed, wiping her eyes with the tissue. "Yeah. Yeah, it is," she said, and then took a deep breath. "But I'm not helping solve her case by getting emotional."

"Getting emotional only proves you care," he said.

"Thank you," she replied with a watery smile. "But now I've got to suck it up and be professional."

"Mary, you don't have to…" he began.

She placed her hand on his chest and looked up at him. "I'm good," she said. "Really."

Nodding, he moved to her side and they both faced the crime scene again.

Alex stepped over the few rows of corn that separated them and walked over to Mary. "What you did today," he said. "Finding her. Telling us about her. Without your help, I don't think her body would have been found until next spring when the farmer came back in the field. And then most of the evidence would have been destroyed, even if her death was accidental."

"I don't think it was an accident," Mary said. "I think she was murdered."

Alex folded his arms over his chest and nodded at her. "Okay, I'm listening," he said. "Why are we opening up a homicide case on this one rather than an accidental shooting?"

"Well, she said with the super moon it was pretty bright outside," Mary replied. "And the deer had run to the road several minutes before she was shot." She paused and collected her thoughts. Think like a cop, she told herself. "The bullet wound looks like it was mid-chest. With her light-colored sweatshirt, it would have been easy to see that a person was in the field, not a deer."

"Okay, all valid points," Alex said and then turned to Bradley. "Do you mind if I work this case with you?" he asked. "Although we need more evidence, I'm beginning to agree with Mary; Ruth McCredie was murdered."

"I'll be happy to have you on the case," Bradley said, and then turned to Mary. "Can you drive yourself home?"

She nodded. "Yeah, I'm pregnant and emotional," she teased, trying to summon a smile, "not incapacitated."

"Are you sure?" Alex asked. "Because I could always drive your…" He looked over to the cemetery and saw a vehicle parked there, but because of the fencing and brush between the field and the cemetery, could not tell what kind it was. "That's not a mini-van, right?"

A real giggle burst from Mary's lips and she shook her head. "No, it's not a minivan," she replied. "And I'm sure, I can drive myself home. You're safe, Alex. No one will see you driving a mom car."

He smiled at her. "You know, for you I would drive it," he replied.

"Yes, I know," she said. "And thank you."

The ambulance pulled behind Bradley's cruiser, and the EMTs hurried to the back to unload the stretcher. Bradley turned to Alex. "Would you direct them while I walk Mary back to her car?" he asked.

"No problem," Alex said. "If you have a brush and a camera, we could try to get rid of some of this snow and see if we can locate any frozen footprints."

"Good idea," Bradley said. "Why don't you guide the EMTs around the long way, just so they don't disturb the area."

Taking Mary's elbow to help her over the uneven ground, Bradley guided her away from the crime scene. "Are you sure you're okay?" he asked. "You're not just putting on a show for Alex?"

"Yes," she replied, shaking her head impatiently. "Even though, you must realize, that my greatest goal in life is to impress Alex."

Bradley chuckled. "Mary, all you have to do is breathe to impress Alex," he said. "I can guarantee that he would have never offered to drive a mom car for anyone but you. I'm afraid the man is completely and utterly smitten."

She stopped at the car and turned to him. "Really? Smitten?" she asked.

He met her eyes. "Of course," he said, lowering his voice. "But don't you forget who is coming home to you tonight."

Smiling up at him, love shining in her eyes, she shook her head. "Oh, don't worry," she said. "I could never forget that."

31

He bent down, kissed her lightly and then leaned against the car. "When you get home," he said. "I'd prefer if you kept the doors locked."

"Why?" she asked.

He slowly scanned the area and then looked back at Mary. "This is not one of your usual cases," he replied, keeping his voice low. "Ruth was killed recently, and you've been spending quite a bit of time in his area. You could have already piqued the killer's interest. Now that her body has been found, we're going to have a killer out there who is going to be trying to cover his tracks. I'd just rather have you overcautious and secure."

"Okay," she said. "I'll make sure I'm careful."

He kissed her one more time. "Good," he said. "I'll see you soon."

He walked away and Mary slipped into the car and started it up. "Okay, Ruth," she said aloud. "Now we've got to figure out who killed you and why."

Chapter Six

It felt strange to turn the lock on the deadbolt in the middle of the day, but Bradley's words of caution kept running through her mind. Could someone have been watching her during her trips to the cemetery? Could she have aroused their suspicion? Was her family in danger?

She heard a noise, and her heart accelerated. Then she saw Lucky jumping from the couch onto the coffee table, knocking the magazines onto the floor. Shaking her head, she took a calming breath and started walking into the living room.

"Boo!"

"Ahhhhhh!" Mary's scream echoed throughout the room as she turned to face the intruder.

"Mary! Wait! It's just me," Mike yelled.

At the sound of his voice, Mary leaned back against the wall, her breath coming out in gasps and her hand on her chest. "Mike," she wheezed. "Oh, Mike. You scared me."

He hovered closer, concerned about her suddenly pallid complexion. "I am so sorry," he said. "I was just teasing. I never meant…"

Still breathless, she shook her head. "No. No," she stammered. "Not your fault. I'm…I'm just a little jumpy."

"You need to sit down," he insisted, hovering around her like a worried mother hen. He shook his head. "After this, I need to sit down."

That comment brought a smile to her face and, after taking one last, unsteady breath, she stood, walked over to the nearest chair and sat down. Lucky jumped up into her lap and started purring. Mary began to stroke the cat automatically.

"Now," Mike said, kneeling down next to her, "tell me what happened. You never act like this."

"When I was out at the cemetery this morning, I found a dead body," she said.

He stared at her for a moment. "But aren't there lots of dead bodies in a cemetery?" he asked. "Isn't that, like, the point of a cemetery?"

"No. I mean, yes, that's the point of a cemetery," she explained. "But, it wasn't one of those kinds of bodies, and to be exact, the body was in the field next to the cemetery." She paused to catch her breath. "Mike, a young woman was murdered and I found her body."

"Mary, that must have been awful for you," he said.

She nodded and clasped her hands together, but Lucky batted at her hand until she began petting her again. "I know I've seen dead bodies before. When I was a cop, I worked homicide," she said. "But for some reason, this was different. I can't seem to calm down."

"What do you mean?" he asked.

"It feels like my heart is racing, and my nerves are on edge," she replied. "I feel like I can't catch my breath, and I feel like the room is closing in around me." She glanced at him, her eyes round with fear. "I don't think I've ever felt this way before."

"Call Gracie," Mike said, referring to Mary's friend and a psychologist for the Chicago Police Department.

"I can't do that," Mary argued.

"If you had a broken arm, would you go see your physician?" Mike asked.

Mary shrugged. "Yes, but…"

Mike sat up on his knees so he was face to face with Mary. "Listen, you've been through a lot in a couple of years," he said adamantly. "Just like your bones and muscles, your mind can get a little bumped and bruised, too. And you need to talk to a professional when something like that happens. Call Gracie."

She thought about it for a moment. It really did make sense. Besides, what was the harm? Gracie would probably just tell her she was over-hormonal and to take a nap.

"Fine," she said, pulling out her cell phone and accessing Gracie's number. "I will."

"Gracie Williams," her friend's familiar voice answered on the first ring.

"Hi, Gracie. It's Mary," Mary said.

"Girl. How are you doing?" Gracie asked. "You haven't had that baby yet, have you?"

Mary smiled and shook her head. "No, he's still a big lump. He's not due until January."

"It sure seems like you've been pregnant forever," Gracie replied.

"Tell me about it," Mary said while Gracie chuckled on the other end of the line.

"What can I do for you, honey?" she asked.

"I don't know," Mary said, feeling a little foolish. "Maybe it's nothing."

"Or maybe it's something," Gracie inserted. "What's going on?"

Taking a deep breath and receiving an encouraging look from Mike, Mary nodded. "Okay, so today I found the body of a young woman in a field outside of town," she began.

"See, I told you those rural towns were scary," Gracie replied. "You need to get yourself back to the big city."

Mary chuckled and felt a little better, but the tension was still there. "Gracie, the young woman had been murdered," she continued. "Bradley suggested that I lock the doors when I got home because I was out near that field a number of times in the past few weeks. If the murderer was watching the area, that he or she might think I knew something."

"So, your handsome police chief was protecting you," Gracie replied. "That's not unusual."

"You're right," Mary said. "He's generally overly protective."

"And you generally roll your eyes and do what you damn well please."

Nodding her head slowly, Mary smiled. "Well, yes, that's true."

"So, what's different?" Gracie asked.

Chapter Seven

Mary paused for a moment to collect her thoughts. What was different? Why was she reacting this way?

"This time, I took his words seriously," she said slowly. "All the way home I worried about someone waiting for me. I was actually panicking from the idea of a stranger watching me, waiting for me. When I got home, I locked the door, and I was jumpier than I've ever been. More than jumpy, almost paranoid."

"Like you were having an anxiety attack, maybe?" Gracie asked.

"Does an anxiety attack feel like you're scared to death and losing control all at the same time?" Mary asked.

"Yes. Yes, it does," Gracie replied.

"Okay, then. Yes," Mary said. "I could have been having an anxiety attack. Is there something wrong with me?"

"Honey, are you sitting down?" Gracie asked.

Mary could feel tension returning to her body. She picked up the cat and placed it on the floor, preparing herself for the worst. "Yes, I'm sitting," she replied, her voice tight.

"Well, honey, first of all, you're pregnant," Gracie said.

Mary released her held breath. "I know that," she said.

"You're pregnant and you're vulnerable," Gracie said. "You're not as fast or flexible as you used to be. You're a bigger target, if you'll excuse my bluntness, and you have a little person inside of you that you need to protect. The danger isn't just about you anymore. It's also about your baby, so you are going to react differently."

Eyes widening, Mary nodded. "Okay, well, that makes sense."

"And you have hormones playing with your emotions when you're pregnant," Gracie continued. "Which is why you often cry or laugh more than you used to. You react with a greater amount of emotion when you're pregnant, and fear is an emotion."

Mary breathed a sigh of relief. "Well, if that's all…" she began.

"Oh, honey, that's not all," Gracie said. "Within the past three years you have experienced trauma to your mental health that most people don't experience in a lifetime. When was the last time you actually found a murder victim when you weren't specifically looking for one? When you hadn't already prepared yourself emotionally for finding a body?"

"I don't know," Mary said. "I guess not since I was on the force."

"So, you just experienced another emotional trauma," Gracie said. "And now that you're not a police officer, finding a body is not routine. There are a lot of feelings swirling around inside you."

Mary thought about the emotional reaction she had at the scene of the crime and nodded. "Yes, I did react emotionally," she admitted. "So, am I messed up? Mentally?"

Gracie's soft chuckle eased Mary's mind. "Oh, honey, we're all messed up," Gracie said. "But you're no more messed up than me."

"So what do I do?" Mary asked. "I can't walk around being afraid all the time."

"That's right. You can't," Gracie replied. "So don't."

"What?"

"Don't walk around being afraid all the time," Gracie said. "Walk around being normal. Get yourself busy with your life, your family, your job, and all the things you love to do. Don't let fear paralyze you. You can make that choice."

"I can?"

"Honey, anxiety isn't a disease. It's a reaction," Gracie explained. "When we worry, stress and are afraid, we create anxiety. Let me ask you, do you know if the murderer is watching you?"

"No, I don't."

"Do you know if the murderer is somewhere in Illinois?" Gracie asked.

Mary shrugged. "I guess I don't know that either," she said.

"So, why are you living with fear in your life when you might not have anything to be afraid of?" Gracie asked. "If you pay attention to your surroundings, if you're practicing situational awareness as you've been trained, what do you have to fear?"

Taking a deep breath, Mary released it slowly. "Nothing," she said.

"You need to get busy with your life," Gracie said. "That's my professional prescription. You make some calls, you do some holiday shopping and you get on with your life. And if you get those feelings again, take a deep breath and realize that it's just an emotional reaction. And you can deal with it because you are one damn strong lady."

"Thank you, Gracie," Mary replied. "You always know just what I need to hear."

"Oh, honey, that's why they pay me the big bucks," she teased. "I love you. You take care of yourself, hear?"

"I hear," Mary said. "And thank you, again."

"You're welcome," Gracie said. "Now call your momma. She'll help you get your life back to normal."

Mary laughed. "You're exactly right," she agreed. "I will."

Chapter Eight

Alex Boettcher watched as the ambulance pulled away from the edge of the road and turned around towards Highway 20. There was no need for a siren or flashing light. Rushing to the hospital would not help their passenger this time.

"You okay?" Bradley asked, standing up and brushing snow and dirt off the knees of his pants. The yellow crime scene tape had been secured by small wooden stakes, and Bradley had just hammered the last stake into the cold, partially frozen ground.

"Sometimes I hate my job," Alex replied softly.

Understanding immediately, Bradley nodded. "I got a call from Dorothy at the station. Ruth's parents live up near Winslow. Do you want to call them?"

"No," Alex said with a long sigh. "I can drive up to Winslow in twenty minutes. The least I can do is deliver the news in person."

"Want some company?" Bradley offered.

Alex looked over at his friend and nodded. "Yeah, actually, I would," he said. "Thank you."

"No problem. I'll let Dorothy know where I'm going," Bradley replied. "Let's take my car. It looks more official than your little sports car."

"Good," Alex replied, with a half-smile. "Then I won't get my car muddy from the gravel roads."

Understanding Alex's need to try and interject a little humor into the depressing situation, Bradley mustered a small smile. "Because we both know mud on your baby would break your heart."

The levity fell flat, and with a sigh, both men walked away from the crime scene towards the road. Before they reached the cruiser, Alex stopped and turned to Bradley. "Okay, I have a question for you."

"Shoot," Bradley replied.

Alex studied his friend for a few moments and finally spoke. "When the EMTs lifted the body, there was a bloodstain on the front of her sweatshirt, just as Mary described," he said slowly. "We both know that Mary didn't disturb the body before she called us. And, with the snow covering and the way Ruth fell when she was shot, there's no way Mary could have seen the stain."

Bradley continued to meet his friend's eyes, but didn't say anything.

"Damn it, Alden, you're going to make this hard on me, aren't you?" Alex growled.

"Make what hard on you?" Bradley replied, feigning innocence.

"How does she do it?" Alex said. "How does she know this stuff?"

Bradley studied his friend for a few more moments and then nodded. "You really want to know?" he asked.

"I think I need to know," Alex said.

"A couple of years ago, Mary was a cop in Chicago," Bradley began.

Alex nodded. "Yeah, I think I knew that."

"They were at a drug bust, and one of the perps was trying to escape. He had a gun and turned and aimed at Sean, Mary's brother. Mary saw it and stepped between the bullet and her brother."

Alex exhaled sharply. "Not many people would do that, even for their family."

"Not many people are like Mary," Bradley replied easily. "She was rushed to Cook County with a bullet wound to the stomach."

"Damn, gut shot," Alex whispered.

"Yeah, painful and…deadly," Bradley replied. He took a deep breath and continued. "She actually died."

Pausing for a moment, Bradley looked out across the field while he regained his composure. Then he cleared his throat and tried again. "She died on the operating table. The trauma to her organs was too much."

"Wait. What? She died?" Alex exclaimed.

"She remembers going toward a light," Bradley continued. "She remembers it was peaceful and all the pain was gone. She felt safe, secure and loved."

He looked at Alex. "I had a similar experience about a year ago," he related. "And I can tell you that it's really hard to come back."

"So, why did she?" Alex asked.

"She heard someone call her name and give her a choice," he said. "She was told that she could continue on if she wanted, or she could go back and be with her family. But, if she chose to go back, things would be different. She would have a different calling."

A truck rumbled by on Highway 20, and both men paused to watch it pass by. Then Bradley continued. "She was able to look back, down on her family waiting in the hospital lobby," he said. "She watched her father fight back tears, her mother sobbing and her brothers anxiously awaiting news. And she knew, no matter how wonderful the light might have been, she had to go back and be with her family. She couldn't let her brother live with the guilt of her death. So, she made her choice."

"When she recovered, she soon discovered what changed in her life," he continued. "She knew there would be a difference. But she had no idea that she would now be able to see and talk to ghosts."

"But there's no such thing…" Alex automatically began and then he stopped. "Okay, that was dumb."

Bradley smiled. "Yeah, well, she gets that a lot," he said. "But the truth is, whether we want to believe or not, there are ghosts. They are real. Most are just regular people who have died and are stuck here on earth until someone can help them get their unfinished business taken care of. Then they get to go to the light. That's what she does, helps them move on."

"So, she sees them…" Alex began.

"In the state in which they died," Bradley said. "Which can be pretty damn gross at times."

"Wait. You've seen them, too?"

"Only with Mary's help," Bradley said. "And let me tell you. The first time I thought I was losing my mind." He smiled sheepishly. "Sometimes I still think I'm living in the Twilight Zone."

"So, Ruth, talked to Mary?" Alex asked.

Nodding, Bradley began walking towards the car with Alex at his side. "Yeah, most ghosts don't even realize their dead," he said. "They're confused, and they are kind of tethered to the site of their death. Now that Ruth knows she's dead, she can leave her physical body."

Alex looked startled. "But what if she never comes back?" he said. "What if she doesn't reappear to Mary?"

"Most of the time they just need a little time to reconcile themselves to what happened," Bradley replied. "Then they appear to Mary, and she's able to help them. Ruth just needs a little time to come to terms with what happened. Then she'll be back."

"How do they…the ghosts…feel about moving on?" Alex asked.

"That's the best part," Bradley said. "Once they see the light, they want to go. Mary once told me she felt like she was going home when she was going towards it."

Alex stopped and slowly looked around the area. "Why was Mary out here?" he finally asked.

"There's a mass grave in the cemetery with a number of ghosts that still haven't moved on," Bradley replied easily.

Straightening, Alex stared at the cemetery. "There are ghosts over there?" he asked.

Bradley grinned. "Lots of them," he said, lowering his voice. "And there may be some standing next to us, right now."

The wind blew, rustling some of the dead vegetation around them, and Alex jumped. "Okay, Alden, I'm officially creeped out," he said, hurrying toward the cruiser. "Let's get out of here."

Once they were inside the vehicle, Alex turned to Bradley. "So, how's your budget for consultants?" he asked.

"What budget?" Bradley replied. "What consultants?"

Alex chuckled. "Yeah, that's what I thought. Listen, I have a line item in my budget for consultants. I don't usually use it; we just roll it over year to year. But I'd like to hire Mary as a consultant on this case."

Bradley shook his head. "Alex, Mary's on the case," he said. "You don't have to pay her."

"I know she's on the case," Alex said. "Because that's the kind of person she is. But I want to pay her. And I believe she's worth every penny."

Bradley put the key in the ignition and turned on the cruiser. "Well, I don't know if she'll accept it."

Alex slipped his seatbelt into place and leaned back in the seat. "Why don't you just let me handle that," he said. "I'll have a contract waiting at her office first thing in the morning."

Putting the cruiser in gear, Bradley made a U-turn towards Highway 20. "Well, good luck with that."

"I don't need luck," Alex teased. "I've got skill."

Chapter Nine

"Hello, my name is Bradley Alden and I'm the chief of police in Freeport," Bradley said to the slight woman who answered the door on the farm in rural Winslow. "This is Alex Boettcher, Stephenson County District Attorney. May we speak with you for a few minutes?"

The woman's hands visibly shook as she unlatched the screen door and stepped back, inviting them into her home. "Is this about Ruth?" she asked, her eyes wide with fear.

"Is your husband home?" Alex asked.

"He's…" her voice broke, and she took a deep breath. "He's out back in the barn. I can get him."

Bradley gently placed his hand on the woman's arm to stop her. "I can get him," he said. "But, if you wouldn't mind, I'd love a hot cup of coffee."

"Oh, yes, I can make coffee," she replied, eager to be busy.

"Thank you," he said. "I'll be right back."

Bradley left the house, and the woman hurried into her kitchen. Alex looked around the room, feeling his anger toward the unknown assailant grow. The room was nearly a shrine to a beloved daughter. Photographs, ribbons and trophies lined the walls and shelves. Ruth with her arms around a prize-winning calf, Ruth standing with her parents next to their tractor, and Ruth sitting in the backseat of a convertible waving to the crowds with a sash that proclaimed her the Winslow River Days Queen.

He walked across the room and picked up the framed photo of her at the parade. "She's beautiful, my little girl."

Alex turned to see Ruth's father just inside the door, his overalls covered with mechanical grease, his rubber boots covered with mud. Bradley stood behind him, closing the door softly.

"Yes, she is," Alex replied, placing the photo back on the shelf. Then he glanced around the room. "And talented, too."

The man's sad eyes sparkled for a moment, and Alex couldn't tell if it was from tears or pride. "Yes, she's quick as a whip."

The man sighed deeply. "You needed to talk to us?" he asked.

Alex nodded.

"I'll get Gloria," Ruth's father said. "Why don't you two sit down."

Bradley and Alex remained standing and waited for Ruth's parents to come back into the room. "I've got the water boiling," she said to Bradley. "It won't take a moment more for me to make your coffee."

"Why don't you sit down, Mrs. McCredie," Bradley suggested softly. "The coffee can wait."

He guided them both to the couch, and then he and Alex sat across from them on stiff-backed wooden chairs.

Tears slipped slowly down the mother's face as she faced the men. "You've found our Ruth?" It was more a statement than a question.

Alex nodded. "Yes, we did," he replied. "This morning." He searched for words that might comfort, that might heal. But he found nothing. "I'm so sorry," was all he could say.

Mrs. McCredie collapsed against her husband, her sobs echoing in the small room. Mr. McCredie patted her gently on her back as he wiped ineffectually at the tears flowing down his wind-worn face. "She was always a good girl," he said, his voice cracking with emotion. "We knew she weren't no runaway. We always knew if she could, she woulda come back home."

Alex nodded. "You're right," he said. "She would have come back home."

Mr. McCredie took a deep catching breath. "How did she…" he began, and then sobbed softly, unable to continue.

"She was shot," Alex said. "In a field just outside of Freeport."

"Shot?" Mr. McCredie asked, incredulous. "Who in the world would want to shoot my little girl?"

"That's what we're going to find out," Bradley said, reaching over and placing his hand over Mrs. McCredie's hand. "I promise you, we will find whoever did this to your daughter."

Mrs. McCredie looked up, her face blotched and tear-swollen. "Can we see her?" she stammered. "Can I see my baby?"

Bradley nodded. "Yes, of course you can," he said. "I'll have Dorothy, my assistant, set things up for you. And if there is anything you need, any questions, please don't hesitate to call my office."

Mrs. McCredie nodded. "Thank you," she whispered. "Thank you so much."

"Is there someone we can call for you?" Alex asked. "A family member or a pastor?"

Mr. McCredie shook his head. "No, I think we've been kind of expecting your visit," he replied. "But it's harder than I thought."

"Yes, nothing can ever prepare us to lose a loved one," Bradley said.

"She was such a good girl," Mrs. McCredie whispered and then turned once again into her husband's arms, her sobs racking her small frame.

Alex met Mr. McCredie's eyes. "It will probably be reported on the news this evening," he said. "I haven't released her name, but now that we've spoken…"

Nodding slowly, Mr. McCredie patted his face with his wet handkerchief. "Well, there's been lots of folks praying for our Ruthie, so it's fitting they know she's been found," he said softly.

Alex placed his card on the coffee table. "Please let me know if there is anything we can do for you," he said, echoing Bradley's words.

"Thank you," Mr. McCredie said, his voice unsteady. "I think, right now, we just need to be alone."

"I understand," Bradley said, standing up. He excused himself for a moment and hurried into the kitchen to turn off the water on the stove. Then he pulled a paper towel off the roll and wiped his eyes, erasing any sign of tears.

When Bradley reentered the room, Alex was already standing next to the door ready to go. Bradley looked down at the couple, wanting to say something, anything that would give comfort. But he knew there was nothing he could say. "I'm so sorry," he finally whispered, his voice catching. "I'm just so sorry."

Chapter Ten

"Hi, Ma," Mary said when her mother answered the phone.

"Mary, what's wrong?" her mother replied immediately.

Tears welled up in Mary's eyes as emotions she didn't realize she'd been holding in began to overflow. "I've had a kind of challenging day," she said, trying to keep the emotion out of her voice. "And I just wanted to talk to you."

"Well, why don't you just tell me about it?" Margaret O'Reilly said softly.

"I found a young woman's body today," she said, and then her voice cracked and the tears began in earnest. "She was so young. She was in college. Someone just shot her, Ma. They just shot her and left her body in the middle of a cornfield."

"But you found her," Margaret said.

Wiping the tears from her cheeks with her hands, Mary nodded. "Yes, I found her," she said.

"And you spoke with her?" Margaret asked.

Mary took a deep, shuddering breath. "Yes, I spoke with her," she replied.

"And you calmed her fears?"

"I had to tell her she was dead," Mary replied. "And she cried. She didn't understand. I don't understand."

"No, there's no understanding hate and cruelty," Margaret agreed. "There's no understanding a heart that can kill so easily."

"It frightened me," Mary admitted. "Standing in the open field. Thinking about her murderer, I was frightened."

"There's no shame in being afraid," Margaret said. "It's what you do about it that shows who you are. What did you do when you found her body?"

"I called Bradley," Mary said.

"And did you leave her body in the field and run away?"

"No, of course not. I stayed with her," Mary said.

"And when Bradley came, did you leave then?" Margaret asked.

"No, I stayed and answered questions so they could find out who did this to her."

"And when were you afraid?" Margaret asked.

"When I got home," Mary said. "Once I locked the doors."

Margaret chuckled wryly. "You are so much like me, Mary," she said. "Brave when we need to be, and then we collapse when no one can see."

Mary was astonished. Her mother had been her solid rock all throughout her life. No one was braver than Margaret O'Reilly. "You've never been afraid, Ma," she said.

"I've never let you see me be afraid," she said. "I couldn't let my children see my fear. I couldn't cause them to be fearful."

Mary shook her head, and then she realized the truth. "Your bathroom," Mary said. "You used to say you needed a moment, and then you'd go into your bathroom."

"And there's the truth of it," Margaret said. "I'd turn on the sink full power and sink to my knees and cry my fears away. I'd say a prayer for strength and protection, slap cold water on my face, and come out and deal with the world."

"I have never been as frightened as I was today," Mary confessed.

"Well, you've a wee babe you're frightened for," Margaret said. "It's only natural. You just can't let the fear overwhelm you."

"That's what Gracie said," Mary replied.

"Aye, Gracie Williams is a very smart woman," Margaret said. "And I'm sure she told you to concentrate on something normal. So, tell me, how are the plans for Clarissa's party?"

Mary smiled. "They're going great," she said. "Although I might need your help."

"Tell me."

"When she was pregnant with Clarissa, Jeannine started making a quilt," Mary explained. "She never got to finish it. Before she moved on, she asked me to complete it and give it to Clarissa as a gift from her mother. I just remembered about the quilt this morning. Can you help me?"

There was silence for a moment on the other end of the line.

"And have you considered asking Jeannine's mother if she'd like to help finish the quilt her daughter started?" Margaret asked.

"No, actually, I hadn't considered it," Mary confessed. "But, Ma, every time I've tried to call her, she doesn't answer the phone, and she doesn't return my messages. I don't know what else I can do."

There was silence on the line as Margaret thought of the right way to answer her daughter and not feel anger towards a woman who was obviously shutting out her daughter's efforts at reconciliation.

"Well, grief is a harder journey for some," Margaret finally said. "And we need to respect her wishes. Is she coming to the party?"

Mary shrugged. "I don't know," she said. "They haven't responded yet."

"Well, don't worry about that," Margaret said brightly. "It will all work out. Tell me, do you have a quilting frame?"

"They have frames?" Mary asked. "I thought it was supposed to be a blanket."

Margaret laughed. "Why don't you call your neighbor, Katie Brennan, and ask her if she has a quilt frame. If not, I'll bring mine. I'm sure it's still up in the attic."

"Ma, do you consider me a complete failure?" Mary asked. "I can't sew, quilt or do crafts."

"Mary you are a miracle, and I thank the good Lord for you every day," her mother replied sincerely.

"I love you, Ma," Mary said softly.

"And I love you, too, Mary-Mary," her mother replied. "Now, go and call Katie Brennan so we can finish that quilt."

Chapter Eleven

"Hi Katie. It's Mary," Mary said.

"Hi, Mary," Katie said pleasantly and then her voice changed. "Oh, no! Is it time? Do you need me to take you to the hospital?"

Mary felt some of her tension dissolve, and she smiled into the phone. "No, I'm good," she replied. "I just have to ask you a potentially odd question."

"Yes?" Katie replied.

"Do you have a quilt frame?" Mary asked hesitantly.

"Yes, do you need it?" Katie asked.

"Well of course you do," Mary chuckled. "You are my official hero."

"Because I have a quilting frame?"

"Something like that," Mary said. "And, yes, I would love to borrow it. Thank you so much!"

Katie chuckled softly. "Well, how can I say no to the woman who is offering me a Thanksgiving dinner where I don't have to cook everything and I only have to help clean up?"

"Really? You don't mind sharing Thanksgiving with us?" Mary asked.

"I love the idea," Katie replied. "Thanksgiving is all about family and friends. Besides, we wouldn't miss the surprise birthday party for Clarissa for the world."

Mary breathed a sigh of relief. "Thank you," she said. "This has been quite a year for her…"

"Quite a year for all of you," Katie inserted.

"That's true," Mary agreed. "But I wanted this birthday, the first one she's having with Bradley, to be extra special."

"Well, if it isn't enough to be born on Thanksgiving," Katie said, "having all of your friends and family share it with you will be very special." She paused for just a moment. "So, what else can I do for you, because I know your plate is always too full. Why do you need a quilting frame?"

Mary sighed. "Okay, you asked for it. There's a baby quilt that I've had in my closet for several months," Mary explained. "It was the quilt Jeannine began when she was pregnant. It was her last gift to Clarissa. It's about half done. She never got to finish it. I thought…"

"That would be a beautiful gift," Katie said softly.

"I called my mom, and she's going to help. I just don't even know where to begin," Mary admitted. "I don't even know if there's enough time between now and Thanksgiving to complete it."

"I'll bring it right over. But where can we set it up and keep it secret?"

It took Mary only a moment to decide. "The new nursery," she said. "We've been slowly getting it ready for Mikey. We can put it in there."

"Okay, I can bring it over now before the kids are all home," Katie said. "It will only take me a few minutes to set it up."

"Are you sure?" Mary asked.

"Then I'll come over later tonight and help you pin the quilt to the frame," she replied.

"Thank you, Katie."

"Mary, that's what friends are for."

Chapter Twelve

Bradley parked the cruiser in the driveway and took a moment to look through the windshield at his home. Lights from inside the house were casting a warm glow on the snow-covered lawn, and he could see shadows of movement inside the house. Exiting the car, he walked quietly, listening to the muffled laughter and conversation coming from inside. He wondered what kind of sounds were coming from the inside of the McCredie home that night.

Taking a deep breath of the chilling air, he hurried up the steps and into the warmth of his home.

"Daddy!" Clarissa yelled and dashed across the room to throw herself into her father's arms.

Bradley knelt down and embraced her, holding her there safely and securely, knowing another man would never be able to do the same with his own daughter. "I love you, baby," he whispered to Clarissa. "With all my heart."

"I love you, too, Daddy," Clarissa replied, a touch of confusion in her voice. "Are you sad?"

Mary walked into the room just in time to hear her daughter's question and see the bleak expression on Bradley's face. Her heart ached for him, and she hurried across the room. "Bradley?" she asked.

He looked up at her, and with Clarissa in his arms, stood and pulled Mary into his embrace. "I'm so glad to be home," he said simply.

"The McCredies?" Mary asked.

He nodded. "They are good people," he replied, his voice catching. "And they loved their daughter. She was everything to them."

"Oh, Bradley," Mary whispered, tears filling her eyes. "I'm so sorry."

He took a deep breath and nodded. "I'm good. I'll be fine," he finally said. "I just needed to hold my family."

He leaned over and placed a kiss on the top of Clarissa's head. "How was your day, sweetheart?" he asked.

She smiled up at him. "I had a great day," she replied. "We got to draw hand turkeys and color them." She held up a slightly paint-spackled hand. "See?"

"She decided to use permanent markers to paint her turkey," Mary explained with a smile. "So, it's going to take a number of hand washings to get all the color off."

"I think your hand looks beautiful," he said. "And I can't wait to see the turkey."

"My teacher hung my turkey up on the bulletin board," Clarissa said. "But she said I can bring it home for Thanksgiving."

Bradley squeezed her and then placed her on the ground. "Well, we will have to tape it on the front window so the whole neighborhood can see your turkey," he said.

"Really?" Clarissa asked, looking from Bradley to Mary.

"Really," Mary replied. "I was wondering how to decorate the front window for Thanksgiving, and your turkey is the perfect solution."

Clarissa was thoughtful for a moment. "Maggie made a turkey, too," she finally said. "Since her family is coming here for Thanksgiving, can she hang her turkey on the window, too?"

"Of course she can," Mary said. "But she needs to be sure her mother doesn't want it for their front window."

"Can I call her and ask?" Clarissa asked.

Mary pulled her cell phone out of her pocket and handed it to Clarissa. "Sure, sweetheart," she replied. "Just don't take too long. Dinner will be ready in about ten minutes."

Phone in hand, Clarissa dashed up the stairs towards her room. Then Mary turned to Bradley. "How are you doing? Really?" she asked.

"Telling the McCredies about Ruth was hard," he confessed. "Even though I knew from the moment we walked in the house they realized she was dead, it was still hard to find the words."

He shook his head. "How do you tell a mother and father that their daughter…" he paused and took a deep breath. "I know…" he began again and cleared his throat. "I know how it feels to have someone you love ripped away from you. One moment you're a nice, normal family. The next moment, everything in your life is changed. The pain is real. And you will never be the same again."

Mary laid her head on his chest and hugged him. "I'm sorry," she whispered softly.

He wrapped his arms around her and placed his head on hers. "Her poor parents," he replied in a hushed voice. "A parent should never have to bury a child. It's not fair."

"No, it's not," she repeated, trying to soothe him. "It's not fair."

Chapter Thirteen

Mary opened the door before Katie could ring the doorbell.

"Clarissa just fell asleep," Mary said to her friend. "I don't want her to wake up and find you here."

"You are so sneaky," Katie teased.

"Well, that's why they pay me the big bucks," Mary teased in return. "So, are you ready to take your life in your hands?"

Katie paused, her eyes wide. "Excuse me?"

Mary grinned. "Oh, you haven't been told about my total lack of crafty prowess," she said.

"It can't be that bad," Katie said.

"Every time I use a sewing machine, I impale my fingers with the needle," Mary confessed. "I can't use a glue gun without getting a third degree burn. And my Pinterest attempts always look like fails."

Katie bit back a laugh. "Come on, Mary," she said. "I've tasted your cooking. You're exaggerating."

Mary shrugged. "Well, I guess you're going to have to see for yourself."

They walked upstairs to the nursery, and Mary pulled out the unfinished quilt to show Katie. "Oh, Mary, it's beautiful," Katie exclaimed, looking at the combinations of squares with vintage floral patterns. "It's like something from a century ago."

Mary stroked the face of the quilt softly. "It's so soft and delicate," she added. "I'm sure Jeannine picked out each piece of fabric knowing it would lay against her baby's tender skin."

Katie took a deep breath to clear the emotion from her voice. "Well, then, we'd better get it finished for Thursday," she said firmly.

It took them about ten minutes to stretch the quilt over the frame. Then Katie sat down next to the frame and gave Mary a quick demonstration on how to hand quilt, pushing the needle and the cotton thread through all three layers of the quilt and then bringing it back up to the top only millimeters away from where it entered.

"Well, that doesn't look too hard," Mary said hesitantly. "Maybe I can do it."

Katie slid out of the seat and offered it to Mary. "It's not hard," she agreed. "But it takes time, because you can't hurry it or you'll get a knot in the thread or create an uneven stitch."

Mary sat down, positioning the chair so her belly didn't hit the frame. She looked up at Katie and smiled. "It seems I'm at a disadvantage already."

71

"Here, let me adjust the frame so it's taller," Katie suggested, moving around the frame and adjusting the legs to better fit Mary's shape. "Now try."

Leaning over, Mary inserted the needle into the layers slowly, then reached underneath the quilt and poked the tip of the needle up through the fabric. "Oh, it's not where it's supposed to be," Mary said, pulling the needle back out. She tried again, but the needle was just slightly off the seam. "This is harder than it looks," she confessed.

"Don't worry," Katie said. "Once you get the hang of it, you'll be awesome."

Mary grinned. "There's that great mom attitude," she chuckled. "A is for awesome. A is for— ouch!" Mary cried out when the needle pricked the end of her finger.

"No, Mary, O is for ouch," Katie teased, handing Mary a piece of tissue paper. "Now make sure you wipe the blood off so it doesn't get on the quilt."

Mary accepted the tissue and blotted the small amount of blood. "Thank you," she said. "Now, let's try this again."

Fifteen minutes later, Mary stretched, her back and neck muscles feeling tight, and looked at the relatively small progress she had made. "How long do I have to do this?" she asked. "A year, right?"

"You're doing great," Katie said. "And now that you've gotten the hang of it, I'll pull up a chair and start on the other side."

Just as she was sitting down, Katie's cell phone rang. "What in the world…" she muttered, pulling the phone from her purse and answering it. "Hi. What's up?"

After a few moments of listening to the other end of the conversation, Katie shook her head. "Well, of course, I understand," she replied and looked over to Mary with regret. "Yes, I'll be home in a few minutes. Bye."

She hung up her phone and shook her head. "I'm sorry," she said. "Clifford just got a call from work. One of the systems went down, and he has to go in. So, I have to go home."

Mary's heart sank slightly, but she realized that Katie had to go home. "Of course," Mary said. "Thank you so much for showing me how to do this. I'll keep practicing, and you will be amazed at what I've accomplished."

"I'll be by to help tomorrow, okay?" Katie asked.

"Perfect," Mary said. She started to push herself up, and Katie stopped her.

73

"I can see myself out," Katie said. "You keep stitching."

Mary relaxed against the chair. "Thanks," she said. "I will."

Mary ran her hand along the delicate row of tiny stitches she'd created. It had taken her another forty minutes, but she could finally see that she was making progress. "Sorry it took me so long, Jeannine," Mary whispered. "But I'll have it done by her birthday."

She rolled her head and stretched, feeling the tension in her muscles. "But I think this is enough for tonight," she continued. "Because I don't think I can even see straight now."

"Whatcha doing?" Mike asked appearing next to her.

Mary jumped and then sighed. "Mike, you really need to stop doing that to me," she said. "You're going to scare me into early labor."

"Sorry, bad habit," he admitted. He looked beyond her. "Pink? Mary, that blanket is pink," he said. "Mikey can't have a pink blanket; he's going to be a manly baby."

Chuckling, Mary shook her head. "It's not for Mikey," she replied. "This is the quilt Jeannine was making when she was pregnant with Clarissa. I promised her that I would finish it." She shrugged slightly. "I thought it might be a good gift from her real mom on her birthday."

Mike leaned over and placed a kiss on Mary's cheek. She could feel the warm brush of air on her skin. "You are an amazing mom, Mary," he said. "And I know this is going to mean a great deal to Clarissa."

Mary shook her head. "Well, thank you, but don't get too carried away," she said. "You don't realize that my sewing skills are less than abysmal. I'm just hoping that quilting will somehow fit into my lack of skill range."

"Well," Mike said with confidence, "if anyone can do it, you can."

Chapter Fourteen

The hallway was dark when Mary stepped out of the nursery. She moved to click on the light, to be sure she didn't trip over Lucky, but the sound of soft sobbing stayed her hand. She listened for a moment and then slowly moved toward the sound, her eyes adjusting to darkness as she moved forward. At the end of the hall, next to a window overlooking their backyard, Mary found Ruth.

"I'm sorry," Ruth cried. "I didn't know where else to go."

"That's perfectly okay," Mary replied, sitting on the window seat near the ghost. "You are welcome here anytime you need me."

"My parents..." Ruth began and then bent her head and sobbed.

"Bradley, my husband, went to see them this afternoon," she said. "And told them they found you."

Ruth nodded. "I know. I was there," she said. Mary saw a blur of movement as Ruth wiped tears away and a small smile appeared on Ruth's face. "He was wonderful. They both were kind, thoughtful and caring. I could hear the pain in their voices. And when Bradley went to the kitchen to turn off the water Mom was boiling, and took a paper towel to blot the tears in his own eyes before he went back into the living room, it brought me to tears."

Mary nodded, her throat too thick with emotion to offer any words.

"They were so nice to my parents," Ruth continued. "But it was still hard to watch Mom and Dad cry like that. I never meant to hurt them."

"You didn't hurt them," Mary insisted. "The person who took your life hurt them. They miss you, and they are mourning the life you could have led. They would give anything to have you back, but they know that's impossible."

"Death sucks," Ruth replied.

Mary bit back the urge to laugh at the irony of the statement and nodded her head. "My grandfather used to say that the only ones who mourn are the ones who were left behind," she said. "But now I wonder if that's true. I can see you're sad, too."

Ruth shrugged. "Well, yeah, I'm sad and more than a little pissed," she replied. "I'd been working on my senior project for over a year. And after getting samples from that final field, I would have had enough information to not only finish the paper, but also probably get it published."

"I wondered why you were out in the field," Mary replied. "So, what kind of samples were you looking for?"

"Ears of corn that had been left behind after harvest," Ruth explained. "I was taking samples from fields where I knew a new kind of seed had been used. My hypothesis was that the chemicals and the bio-engineering they were using with the seeds were transferred through the plant to the fruit and it was ending up in the food chain."

"How did you know that farmer used those seeds?" Mary asked.

Ruth paused and looked away for a moment. Then she turned back to Mary. "I have an internship with Granum," she admitted, naming a large, bio-tech agricultural company in Stephenson County. "I'm working on my degree in bio-engineering. When I was working in the lab, I discovered that the properties they said were water soluble and would eventually be leached out of the plant into the soil actually remained within the plant."

"So people who ate the corn…" Mary began.

Ruth shook her head. "No, most of the corn grown around here is either field corn, which goes into feed for animals, or we use it for ethanol," she interrupted. "And, you know, with the ethanol it's no big deal. Another chemical in a gas tank, who's going to know? But with feed, that's another story. People are eating meat that's laced with chemicals that could make them sick."

"Did you tell anyone?" Mary asked.

Ruth shrugged. "Yeah, my direct supervisor in the lab," she said. "But he just told me that they had already tested the lifespan of the chemicals in the seed and found them to be a negligible risk."

"Was he right?" Mary asked.

Shaking her head, Ruth rolled her eyes. "No, he was just patting me on the head and telling me to behave like a good little intern and toe the line," she said. "But, you know, my family uses that feed. My parents eat that meat. I thought, screw you. I'll do research on my own."

She paused, her eyes widening, and she turned to Mary. "Do you think that's what got me killed?" she asked. "Do you think they found out that I was about to blow the lid on their seeds?"

"Were you?" Mary asked. "About to blow the lid?"

Ruth nodded. "Yeah, I just needed those last samples to corroborate the tests I'd already run," she said. "The proof was already there. I had corn samples, soil samples and meat samples. It was an amazing research paper."

"Where are all your samples and research?" Mary asked.

Ruth smiled. "In my backpack," she replied. "I didn't trust anyone, so I carried everything with me."

"What backpack?" Mary asked.

The smile dropped from her face. "The backpack I had with me when I got shot," she said. "It was right there next to me."

"I didn't see a backpack," Mary replied. "But there was snow on the ground, so it could have been covered over and we just didn't see it."

"Mary, you have to find that backpack," Ruth said.

Mary nodded. "I agree," she said. "And we'll start looking first thing in the morning."

"I'll start looking now," Ruth said as she began to fade away.

Mary watched Ruth disappear from sight and then stood up to find her husband. She had a feeling Bradley wouldn't want to wait for the morning either.

Chapter Fifteen

When Mary opened the door to her bedroom she saw Bradley propped up on pillows, his hands tucked behind his head, chest bare and his cotton pajama bottoms slung low on his waist. His smiled at her, and his eyes sparkled with desire. "I've been waiting for you," he said, his low voice scraping over her nerves, causing her body to shiver. "We have an appointment."

Lust, pure and simple, washed over her body. She could feel her heart accelerating and heat blossom in her body. But then she felt regret as she sighed and shook her head.

His smile dropped. "What's wrong?" he asked, sliding around the bed and sitting on the edge to meet her.

She stood between his legs and placed her hands on his strong, bare shoulders. "Ruth was out in the hallway," she said, remorse accenting her words.

Bradley's hands were slowly unbuttoning Mary's shirt and pausing to caress the silky skin underneath. "So?" he asked softly, leaning forward and pressing his lips to her skin.

Mary shuddered and inhaled sharply, feeling her knees weaken. "So…" she repeated mindlessly.

She shook her head. "So, she was in the field working on a report that could have cost Granum a lot of money."

He continued to nibble on her skin, tracing just above her bra line. "Um, hmmm," he whispered.

Her hands strayed from his shoulders, up his neck and buried themselves in his thick hair. She lifted her head up, eyes closed, and let the heat wash over her as Bradley slipped his hands underneath her shirt and unhooked her bra. "She...," Mary gasped. "She said she had a backpack with her that contained all of the information." She moaned softly as she felt his hands slowly glide across her skin. "She was sure she had it when she was shot."

His hands stopped, and he lifted his head. "What did you say?" he asked, his voice still hoarse.

She took another deep breath and looked down at him. "She had a backpack with her that contained samples and all the evidence she needed to prove that the chemicals Granum was putting in the seeds were continuing on through the plant and then into the animals fed with the seed."

"She's sure she had the backpack?" he asked.

Mary nodded. "That's why she was in the field that night," she explained, "getting some final samples. She was ready to not only prove her thesis, but also publish a paper that could..."

"Ruin the company," Bradley finished and then shook his head. "We didn't find a backpack."

"I know," she said. "But with the snow…"

"And maybe a raccoon could have carried it farther into the field," Bradley added.

He lifted his hand and tenderly stroked the side of her face. "Mary, I…" he began.

She turned her face and kissed the palm of his hand. "I know," she said. "I knew before I walked in the room. I just let you distract me for a few moments."

He grinned. "They were great moments," he said.

Leaning forward she kissed him fully on the lips. "Really great," she sighed.

He pulled her tight and returned the kiss, showing her just how much he regretted leaving.

"I'll try to be quick," he said, placing another quick kiss on her lips before hurrying across the room to his dresser and pulling out clothing.

She grinned, knowing he'd be out all night. "Sure you will," she replied. "But I'll give you a raincheck."

He glanced over his shoulder and smiled at her. "I love you."

"I love you, too," she replied. "So, what can I do to help?"

Pulling a t-shirt over his head, he came across the room and placed his hands on her upper arms. "Get some sleep," he said. "Enough sleep for both of us."

Glancing at the clock, she shrugged. "It's still early," she said. "What if I pack you a lunch? At least then I'll feel a little useful."

"A lunch would be great," he said. "Thank you."

She started walking towards the door when he stopped her. "Um, Mary," he called.

She turned. "Yes?"

"You might want to, um, button things up before you leave the room," he suggested with a wide grin.

She looked down, surprised to find herself more exposed than she realized. "Good grief," she said, readjusting her clothes. "You work fast."

He met her eyes, passion still smoldering in his own. "Unfortunately, tonight I wasn't fast enough."

Chapter Sixteen

Mary awoke the next morning to the sound of her bedroom door opening. She sat up and saw her exhausted husband, his clothing stained with mud and his face lined with small scratches, trying to quietly sneak past her.

"What happened?" she asked.

He looked over at her. "I'm so sorry I woke you," he said. "I was trying to be quiet."

She slipped out of bed and went over to him. "You were very quiet. I'm just a light sleeper these days." She ran her hand lightly over his face. "Ouch, this looks painful," she said. "Did you run into a bramble bush?"

"Yeah, well, those things are hard to see at night," he confessed.

"Come into the bathroom," she insisted, pulling his hand. "Let me clean you up."

His meek obedience told her he was even more exhausted than she initially thought. Gently cleaning the scrapes, she felt her heart fill as she watched him fight to stay awake. Finally satisfied that the cuts were clean, she bent down, kissed his forehead and patted him on the shoulder. "Go to bed, Chief Alden," she ordered.

He shook his head. "No, I'm good," he said. "I just need a little sleep."

She choked back a laugh. "You're right, that's a better idea," she replied. "Why don't you let me help you get undressed?"

He smiled wearily. "Well, that's an offer I certainly won't refuse," he mumbled.

She led him over to the bed. "Okay, you sit here, and I'll get your pajamas," she said and then turned toward the dresser. She had only just pulled open the drawer when she heard the soft sound of a body falling against the mattress and pillow. Shaking her head, she closed the drawer and turned to see Bradley, his feet still planted on the ground, but the upper half of his body cradled in the soft blankets and pillows on their bed. Smiling, she walked over and pulled his boots off his feet and lifted his legs onto the bed. She pulled a blanket from the end of the bed up over him and tucked him in.

"Good night, sweetheart," she whispered, placing a soft kiss on his cheek.

He murmured something unintelligible and continued to sleep.

A little later, Mary was downstairs, dressed for the day, sipping herb tea and waiting for Clarissa to come down.

"How are you doing?" Mike asked as he appeared next to her.

She was pleased to note that she didn't even flinch at his sudden appearance. "Good," she said, surprised at her answer. "I actually think I'm good. I don't feel in the least bit anxious."

"Excellent," he replied. "And to what miraculous event can we attribute your recovery?"

She grinned and shrugged. "I don't know, perhaps the advice of a good friend," she said, sending him a meaningful look. "Or the diagnosis of a brilliant psychologist, or the words of a wise mom."

He chuckled. "Or just getting on with your life and not having the time to fret," he suggested.

She shook her head. "I don't know. I always seem to find the time to fret," she replied. "Is that normal?"

Mike chuckled. "For you, yes," he said. "So, what's on the agenda for today?"

"Well, I think I might take Clarissa out for breakfast this morning so Bradley can get some sleep," she said.

"You two don't make that much noise," Mike replied.

"It's not the noise. It's the smells," Mary said with a smile. "That man can't sleep through the smell of bacon, no matter how tired he is. He would sleep through a house fire, but not bacon."

"That could be a real problem if you ever have a house fire," Mike replied.

"Oh, no, I always keep bacon on hand just for that reason," she teased. "I'll just throw the package on the fire, and he'll be awake in just a few moments."

Chuckling, Mike nodded. "And after breakfast?"

"I'm feeling good enough to go into the office," she said. "I'll probably avoid the cemetery for a few days, just while the police are still out there searching the scene."

"Good idea," Mike said. "Anything I can do to help?"

Mary smiled up at him. "Um, do you know how to quilt?" she asked.

Mike laughed aloud. "Yeah, no such luck," he replied. "But don't worry. I have a strong feeling that the quilt will be done in time."

"From your mouth to God's ears," Mary replied flippantly.

Mike paused and just stared at her for a moment. "Well, actually, that's just the way it works."

Chapter Seventeen

"This is none of your business, Margaret O'Reilly," Margaret O'Reilly said to herself in the rearview mirror of her car as she turned off the main street in Sycamore, Illinois and headed to the address she'd gotten from Bernie Wojchichowski the Cook County coroner.

She pulled up in front of the tidy home and shook her head. "You are sticking your nose where it doesn't belong," she muttered to herself. Then she shook her head. "It matters to your daughter and your granddaughter, so of course it matters to you."

She glanced in the mirror again. "So, we're going to do it?" she asked herself, and then she nodded. "Come hell or high-water."

She exited the car and walked up to the cranberry painted door. She could see the garden area around the front porch was in slight disarray, more neglect than anything else. She spied a number of cobwebs between the banisters, noted the dirt and dust on the windowsills and windows and shook her head. Yes, something needed to be done.

With a determined move, she jabbed her finger against the doorbell and listened with a little trepidation as it echoed through the inside of the house. Moments later she could hear footsteps coming her way. A kindly man about her own age answered the door and looked questioningly at her.

"Hello, Bill. Bill Whitley?" Margaret asked.

The man nodded in assent. "Yes, I'm Bill," he replied.

"You probably don't remember me," she said. "We met a few months ago, at your daughter's funeral."

She saw sadness pass across his features, and she nearly turned away from her purpose. *No!* An inner voice commanded her. *You need to see this through.*

She took a deep breath and continued on. "I'm Margaret O'Reilly," she explained. "My daughter, Mary, helped solve Jeannine's murder."

"She's the woman who married Bradley," he stated.

Margaret nodded. "Yes, she did," she replied. "And she's also the woman who's raising your granddaughter."

Pain replaced sadness, and he nodded. "I understand she's doing a fine job," he replied gently.

Margaret smiled. "She loves Clarissa with all her heart."

He looked at her, silent for a moment. "What can I do for you, Margaret?"

"I need to have a word with you and Joyce," she replied. "It won't take much time, and it's important."

"I appreciate your effort," he replied. "But I don't think it's going to do you any good. Joyce doesn't talk to many people these days."

Margaret nodded. "Bill. May I call you Bill?" she asked.

He nodded.

"Bill, I've just driven nearly two hours from the northwest side of Chicago to speak with you and your wife," she explained. "I prayed half the time and argued with myself the other half. This is not something I easily do. I tend to stay out of other people's business as a rule, but a voice told me that I needed to do this. So, here I am. If Joyce kicks me out, then at least I did all I could."

Bill smiled widely. "You know, Margaret, I think a plain-spoken woman like you might just be what Joyce needs," he said, opening the door wider. "Please come in."

She walked into the house and immediately missed the brightness of the day. All the blinds were closed and the curtains drawn. It was as if the

92

Whitleys were living in a tomb of their own making. Bill led her down the hall to the living room.

"Bill, who was at the door?"

Margaret turned to see a woman ensconced in a large recliner with an afghan covering her lap and legs.

"We have a visitor, Joyce," Bill said in a voice that warned his wife someone was with him.

Joyce turned and looked at Margaret. "I'm sorry," she said. "I don't believe I know you."

Her voice was tight and cold.

"This is Mary O'Reilly, I mean Mary Alden's mother," Bill said gently.

Pain was more evident on Joyce's face than it had been on her husband's. She looked like she'd been struck at the mention of Mary's name. "I really have nothing to say to you or your daughter," Joyce said stiffly. "Now, if you'll—"

"That's fine," Margaret said, her Irish temper slightly ruffled. Mary had done nothing but help. There was no reason to regard her as the enemy. "You may have nothing to say, but I've got quite a bit. And we can begin with this."

She pulled a photo album out of her purse and opened it wide. "This is a recent photograph of your granddaughter, Clarissa," Margaret said, shoving the photo under the woman's nose. "Mary told me she looks just like Jeannine. What do you think?"

Chapter Eighteen

It took just a moment for the woman's surprised eyes to move from Margaret's face reluctantly down to the album. She tried to just quickly glance, but her eyes were drawn back down to the eager, smiling face in the photo. Tears filled her eyes, and her face softened. She lifted her hand and traced a fingertip around the child's face. "Yes," she whispered. "Yes, she does look like Jeannine."

"Do you have any pictures of Jeannine at her age?" Margaret asked. "I would love to see them."

Joyce looked even more surprised, and then she smiled. "Yes, we do," she said, pushing the afghan off her legs. "I'll be just a minute."

She left the room, and Bill came over to Margaret. "May I look at the photo?" he asked.

"Oh, of course you can. I'm so sorry," she replied, handing him the album.

He stared at the photo in amazement. "She looks just like our Jeannine," he said, his voice catching. "It's incredible."

He looked up at Margaret. "Do you know? Does she have a picture of her mother?" he asked. "Or would that be too confusing for a child?"

Just then Joyce came into the room with a stack of albums in her arms. She placed them on the coffee table in the middle of the room and shook her head. "Well, of course that would be confusing," she said sharply. "She's just a child. A child who's been tossed from one home to another. Of course they wouldn't want to let her know her mother was murdered."

Margaret pulled a folded piece of paper from her purse and held it in her hand. "Clarissa's birthday is on Thanksgiving day," she said. "And my gift to her is a memory book, so Mary let me go through some of the papers and pictures she's been saving. Before I left my house this morning, a little voice told me I ought to bring this paper along. It's from a class assignment Clarissa did at the beginning of the school year."

She opened the paper and held it out to Bill and Joyce.

Class assignment: My Family

My family is not like other families. I have three mommies and two daddies. My first mommy loved me very much. She protected me and watched over me. But she died when I was born. I know that she is watching over me from heaven. My first daddy didn't know where I was. He searched and searched for me. But he couldn't find me.

96

My second mommy and daddy adopted me. They loved me, too. They played with me and taught me all kinds of things. They brought me to Freeport. But, when my second daddy died, we had to move. Then my second mommy died, too. I was very sad.

Finally, my first daddy found me. He brought me home to live with him and my third mommy. They love me, too. And I love them. I am lucky to have had so many mommies and daddies. The End.

Joyce looked up from the paper, confused. "They talk to her about Jeannine?" she asked. "They let her know that Jeannine was her mother?"

Margaret nodded. "Yes, they do," she replied. "They want her to know as much about her mother as they can. Jeannine is a part of Clarissa, a special part, and they want her to know that."

Bill handed the paper back to Margaret. "You said that your daughter, Mary, told you that Clarissa looked just like Jeannine," he said. "How did she know that?"

Margaret thought about her answer for a few moments and then, as if answering herself, nodded firmly. "Well, you are members of the family now," she said. "So, I suppose it's only fair that you know."

"Know what?" Joyce asked.

"The story behind Mary and Jeannine's relationship," Margaret said. "Do you mind if I sit down? This might take a little while."

"Please, let's all sit around the dining room table," Bill offered.

Bill and Joyce led her from the living room into the large, formal dining room. Bill pulled out the chair at the head of the table for Margaret. "Could I get you something to drink?" he asked.

"A glass of water would be lovely," Margaret said. "I have a feeling that by the end of this story, my throat will be dry."

A few minutes later, with a glass of water in front of her, Margaret began. "Well, I suppose you could say this all started when Mary died…"

Chapter Nineteen

Mary opened the door to her office and stared at the envelope laying on the floor just beyond the mail slot. Slowly bending over, she picked it up and noticed it was from Alex's office. Opening it, she pulled out the contract and read it over, twice. The sum for consulting was sizable, but Mary wasn't sure she could become an official part of the investigation. What if it caused her anxiety to worsen?

"I thought you were going to be hanging around some cemetery this morning, girlie," came a familiar voice behind her. "Iffen I had known you were coming in, I would have saved you a donut."

Looking over her shoulder, she smiled at Stanley. "Well, things didn't turn out quite the way I thought," she admitted.

"Hey," he said, staring at her face. "Looks to me like things are even worse than that. You got a worried look on your face. Are you okay?"

She nodded and placed the letter in her inbox. "I found the body of a young woman near the cemetery yesterday morning," she explained. "It looks like she was murdered."

"Murdered?" he repeated, astonished. "You found a real body? Not a ghost?"

Suddenly Mary froze. "Stanley, can this conversation wait for just a moment?" she asked urgently. "I really have to go to the bathroom."

Blushing slightly, Stanley nodded. "Yeah. Yeah. You go, and I'll take care of things out here."

After Mary closed the door on the adjoining bathroom, Stanley strolled around the office space, picking up knickknacks and thumbing through a few magazines placed in a basket near Mary's desk. Finally, bored, he began to sift through Mary's inbox, glancing at the correspondence in it. The letter from Alex's office caught his eye, and he picked it up to get a better look.

The bathroom door opened, but Stanley didn't look up from the letter.

"Find something that interested you?" Mary asked, hoping the sarcasm made it through to Stanley.

"Yeah, this letter here is real interesting," he replied simply.

She sighed and shook her head. Nope, she thought, the sarcasm didn't even faze him.

"Did you know that reading another person's mail is a federal offense?" she asked.

Still reading, he shook his head. "No, opening another person's mail is a federal offense," he replied easily. "Reading it, after it's been opened, is just rude and nosy."

Mary snorted softly. "Well, at least you admit it," she said.

Stanley looked at her over the top of the letter. "So, why is the Stephenson County D.A. looking to sign a contract with you?" he asked.

"Alex came with Bradley yesterday when I found the body," she replied with a shrug. "I don't know why he'd want me on the case."

"Because he's a might smarter than I thought he were," Stanley replied. "O' course he wants you on the case. Dadgummit, you can actually speak with the victim. He'd be a fool not to hire you."

She stepped up, took hold of the letter and eased it from his hands. "Stanley, I don't know if I can do this," she said. "This is a current homicide with a murderer running around loose."

Stanley stared at her. "Yeah. So?" he asked.

"It's dangerous," she said.

"Since when have you run away from danger?"

She sighed. "Since yesterday," she admitted. "When I got so overwhelmed I nearly lost it."

He shook his head. "Now listen to me, girlie. You are one of the best private investigators I've ever known, and it ain't got nothing to do with your special gift," he said. "It's got to do with your instinct, your training and your intelligence. And most of your cases pay you squat, diddly and nada. You got a new baby coming. You got a daughter and a husband, and you got bills. So, sometimes you should think about maybe making some real cash."

She sighed and looked down at the letter. "It really is quite a bit of money, isn't it?"

"Couldn't hurt to have a conversation with them," he said, biting back a smile. "And I like the part where it says it's a flat fee. So, you solve the crime in a couple of days, you still get the big payout."

Nodding slowly, she studied the letter once more. "This kind of money could be very helpful," she agreed, and then she looked up at him. "But what if I feel overwhelmed again?"

Stanley shrugged. "All that means is you might need a little help," he said. "I think you could take this one on."

"You're right," she agreed, and then she smiled at him. "Thanks for being rude and nosy."

He chuckled softly. "Just doing what I do best, girlie," he teased. "And now, iffen I happen to have one of those cream-filled chocolate long johns

102

left in the breakroom, you want me to sneak it over here for you?"

She thought about the breakfast she and Clarissa had finished about an hour ago. Actually, she'd just had fruit and toast. She could probably justify a long john. Her smile widened. "That would be amazing," she replied.

"Okay, you make the call to Alex," he said. "And I'll reconnoiter over in our breakroom and see what I can come up with."

Chapter Twenty

Mary slipped into her chair and studied the letter once more. "Do I really want to do this?" she whispered. Then she thought about the money and smiled widely. "Yes. Yes, I really do."

Placing the letter on the desk in front of her, she picked up her cell phone and dialed the number. After a moment, a receptionist answered the phone. "Stephenson County District Attorney," the friendly voice answered. "How can I help you?"

"Hello. May I speak with Alex Boettcher?" Mary asked.

"Certainly," was the reply. "May I ask who's calling?"

"This is Mary O'Reilly-Alden," she replied. "In regards to a letter he sent me."

"Of course. I'll connect you immediately."

After a brief moment on hold, Mary heard the connection on the other end pick up. "Mary," Alex said. "I hope I'm going to be happy to hear from you."

Smiling at his comments, Mary leaned back in her chair, a little more relaxed. "Well, that's an interesting comment," she said.

"Bradley was pretty sure you were going to turn me down," he admitted. "But maybe I shouldn't have said anything about that."

Chuckling, Mary shook her head. "Actually, he didn't talk to me about it at all," she admitted. "But it was kind of a crazy night for him."

"Yeah, I heard about the search," he said. "Any luck?"

She shook her head. "I don't know," she said. "He was too tired to talk about it this morning."

"I wish he would have called me," Alex said. "I would have come out and searched with him and his team."

"But wouldn't that give whoever you prosecute the ability to accuse you of tampering with the evidence?' Mary asked.

"I don't know," Alex replied. "It just depends on who we're going after."

"I think I might have an idea," Mary said.

"Okay, don't say another word until we both sign that contract," he said. "I'll be over in a few minutes."

"Wait. What?" Mary asked. "I don't know if I'm going to—"

"Mary, I need you on my team to solve this crime," Alex said bluntly. "Are you going to turn me down?"

"Well, no, of course not," she stammered. "When you put it that way."

"Good, I'll be over in a couple of minutes," he replied.

"But…" Mary sighed and stared at her phone for a moment when it was obvious that he had disconnected before she was able to stop him. She placed her phone on the top of the desk and leaned back farther in her chair. "Well, I suppose you don't get to be a D.A. without going after what you want."

"You talking to yourself again, girlie?" Stanley asked as he entered the office balancing a long john on a paper plate. He gestured with the plate in her direction. "Lookie what I found."

He sat down in the chair across from her and slid the plate onto her desk.

"Thank you so much," she replied, sitting forward and picking up the long john. Taking a bite, she closed her eyes in ecstasy, relishing the creamy smoothness of the Bavarian cream and the crisp layers of the light doughnut pastry. "This is so good."

"So, why was you talking to yourself?" he asked.

She swallowed and shrugged. "I called Alex, and he was a little more…" she paused to find the right word. "Aggressive. Maybe assertive. I don't know. He stopped me before I could tell him some crucial evidence about the case. Told me I couldn't say a word until I signed the contract. He's on his way now. He really didn't even give me the chance to turn him down."

Stanley's eyes narrowed. "I don't like this, Mary," he said. "Seems a might more than pushy to me. Seems secretive. Maybe you shouldn't have agreed."

Mary nearly choked on the second bite of long john. "Excuse me?" she murmured around the pastry. "Aren't you the one who suggested…no, insisted I call him?"

"Well, maybe I did and maybe I didn't," he replied. "But you need to take precautions. What's going on at the District Attorney's office that makes him want to sign his contract before talking about the case? Sounds a little iffy to me, if you know what I mean."

"I don't think there's anything to it," she said. "I just think he's a slightly overzealous person and he wants to talk to me in person."

Stanley leaned back in the chair, extended his legs and crossed one ankle over the other. "Well, I suppose he's going to be talking to both you and your new assistant," Stanley stated decidedly.

Mary nearly choked again. "My new assistant?" she gasped.

"Yep," he said with a nod. "And I ain't making no coffee."

Chapter Twenty-one

Alex walked through the door to Mary's office with another, older, dark-suited man. Mary could see that he was not pleased with his companion and sent a quick look of apology in Mary's direction. "Hi, Mary," he said. Then he turned to Stanley. "Stanley. Good to see you."

"We'll see if it is or if it ain't," Stanley said. "What did you bring him for?"

Alex rolled his eyes. "Mary, have you ever met our county board president?" he asked.

Mary shook her head and pushed herself out of her chair. "I thought you looked familiar," she said. "But no, I don't think we've ever met in person."

The man cast a quick glance around Mary's humble office and sniffed with disdain. "This is your only office?" he asked.

"Nah, she's got one on Michigan Avenue in Chicago," Stanley inserted before Mary could answer. "But she prefers hanging around with the little people. You know, folks like you."

Biting back a smile, Mary extended her hand. "I'm Mary O'Reilly-Alden," she offered in a voice that held a bit of coolness and reserve. "And you are?"

"Sargent. Montgomery Sargent," the man replied tersely.

"Had a dog named Sargent once," Stanley said. "Stupidest creature ever born. Why that dog would lay in his own—"

"Stanley," Mary interrupted sharply.

With a mild shrug and a grin, Stanley nodded. "Just trying to make small talk," he chuckled.

"Mary," Alex explained, "I met Monty as I was leaving my office. He insisted on coming along."

"No, that's fine," Mary said.

"I'm sure it's more than fine," Monty said to Alex, once again casting his glance around the small office space. "I'm sure she could use the money."

Anger and pride bubbled up inside Mary's chest. "I'm so sorry to have wasted your time," she said evenly, anxious to turn both of them away. "But I've just looked at my calendar, and unfortunately..."

A look of desperation from Alex stopped her, and she sighed. "Unfortunately, I won't be able to start until this afternoon," she finished, the words tasting sour and unpalatable.

"No. That's great," Alex replied, mouthing the words 'thank you.' "This afternoon's just great. Let's sign that contract."

"Not so fast, Boettcher," Montgomery said. "This is the county's money that's paying her fee." He turned to Mary. "Just what kind of credentials do you have?"

"You don't have to do this, girlie," Stanley said.

Mary sighed and shook her head. "No, Stanley, I do," she replied. "I really do."

Bending, she opened the file drawer on her desk and pulled out a large binder. She placed it in the center of the desk, turned it so it faced Montgomery and then opened it up. "Here are a few letters of recommendation, also my rank and classification from the Chicago Police Department," she said. "Please feel free to look through them and I would be happy to answer any questions you have."

Mary smiled inwardly when she saw Montgomery's eyes widen as he read the recommendation from the Illinois senator who used to reside in Galena. He glanced up at her. "You did work for Senator Ryerson?" he asked.

Mary nodded. "Yes, I did," she said simply, letting the very complimentary letter speak for itself.

111

Montgomery turned the page and blanched slightly. "You worked undercover with the Chicago Police Department?" he asked.

She nodded. "It was an internal issue, so they needed a consultant."

He flipped another page. "Sir Ian MacDougal? You know MacDougal?"

She shrugged easily, hiding her satisfaction. "We worked together for several months," she said. "He needed my help with some of the research he was performing."

"I've read about him. He's...he's a millionaire," Montgomery stuttered.

"At least a millionaire," Stanley inserted, a wide smile on his face. "Mary here's been a guest at his castle. You did know he owned a castle, didn't you?"

Montgomery turned to Stanley. "Yes, I knew that," he stated.

Stanley nodded. "He ever invite you to stay there?" he asked, his hairy eyebrows raised.

Montgomery turned away from Stanley and flipped another page of the book.

"Sorry, I didn't quite get your answer," Stanley said, raising his voice slightly. "You ever been to MacDougal Castle?"

"No," Montgomery growled. "I have never been there."

"Well, that's a shame. That's a damn shame," Stanley replied. "Iffen you'd like, I can give Ian a call and ask him for an invite for you. Because I have his private cell number on my phone."

"That won't be necessary," Montgomery replied, his teeth grinding.

"Well, no problem," Stanley said. "I was going to be calling him anyhows to tell him how some uppity county board president was rude to Mary."

"Stanley," Mary chastised him softly. "Stop."

Shaking his head, Montgomery looked at Mary. "No, he's right," he admitted. "I've been an ass. And I do apologize. We would be honored to have you work with us." He held out his hand for Mary to shake.

"Thank you," she replied, her smile warming. "It will be interesting working with you." She turned to Alex. "Now, when do you want to talk about the actual case?"

Chapter Twenty-two

"So, you're saying that Mary put herself in danger in order to solve Jeannine's murder?" Bill asked Margaret.

"Mary's from a long line of law enforcement professionals," Margaret explained. "I think she felt that she was only doing what was right, what she was supposed to do."

Joyce shook her head. "I had no idea," she confessed. "Bradley told us about the kidnapping and Jeannine's death, but I had no idea that Mary had…"

She looked over at Margaret. "I have to admit that I was angry with your daughter," she said quietly. "She was going to marry Jeannine's husband, and they were going to raise Jeannine's child. It wasn't fair."

"No, you're right. It wasn't fair," Margaret acknowledged. "But Mary wasn't responsible for Jeannine's death. She and Jeannine worked together to solve the case, and Jeannine was happy for Mary and Bradley. Jeannine told Mary that she wanted Bradley to be happy and move on with his life."

Margaret took a deep breath and continued. "And I think she'd want both of you to do the same," she said.

Joyce placed her head in her hands and didn't speak for a few moments. Then she looked up, tears running down her cheeks. "It's so easy for you to say it," she sobbed. "You didn't lose a daughter. You have no idea."

Nodding, Margaret met Joyce's eyes. "I can tell you it wasn't easy for me to say it," she replied. "I believe you have the right to grieve in any way you choose. Everyone has to deal with death in their own way. But, the reason I needed to come by today is not about you or about my daughter. It's about Jeannine and her daughter."

"What do you mean?" Bill asked.

"How do you think your daughter feels about her own parents not getting to know Clarissa?" Margaret asked. "You lost your daughter. Why are you throwing away your chance to get to know your granddaughter?"

"I...I didn't think..." Joyce began.

"You have been so caught up in your own grief that you haven't looked around to see others grieving beside you," Margaret stated boldly. "Don't you think that Bradley still grieves for her? Don't you think Clarissa still wonders about her mother?"

Joyce shook her head. "Sure, blame us. Blame me," Joyce cried. "But your daughter never made us welcome. Never really wanted us to come to their home."

Margaret felt her temper rising. She knew Mary had done nothing but welcome both Bill and Joyce. Joyce's comments were totally unwarranted. She closed her eyes for a quick moment and prayed for patience.

When she opened her eyes, she looked at Joyce and saw a woman with a broken heart, who was not only fearful but also consumed in grief. Margaret felt sympathy well up in her heart, and rather than argue, she took a deep breath and stood up, softly pushing her chair away from the table. "I'm sure I've overstayed my welcome," she said, her voice both patient and kind. "And I've probably said more than I should have. So, I'm going to let myself out."

She put the album in the middle of the table. "This is actually an extra copy of photos I already have," she said. "So these are yours to keep. I've also included information about Clarissa's surprise birthday party. Mary and Bradley are celebrating it on Thanksgiving Day. I understand that Mary sent an invitation to you, but perhaps it was lost in the mail."

She placed her hand on Joyce's shoulder. "Thank you for taking the time to speak with me. If you decide to come on Thanksgiving, please know that you will be more than welcomed."

Turning, she walked down the hallway, which seemed much longer this time, and let herself out the door, closing it firmly behind herself. Once she was out in the fresh air, she took a deep breath and strode down the path to her car.

"I only pray I've done more good than harm," she said to herself as she unlocked the door and slipped inside. "And only time will tell."

Chapter Twenty-three

The bell rang above Mary's office door as Bradley entered. His eyes went directly to Mary and he smiled. "Good morning," he said, his voice still a little rough.

"Morning," she replied, smiling back at him. "How are you feeling?"

He grinned and rolled his head. "Like I spent the night in a field," he replied. He lifted his hand to his face. "Thanks for the fussing this morning. It helped."

"You're welcome," she replied. "Why aren't you still sleeping?"

"Lucky decided I'd stayed in bed long enough," he replied. "She was serenading me outside the bedroom door." He sighed. "We have a very determined kitten."

Mary smiled at him. "Sorry," she said.

He shrugged. "It was time to get up anyway," he admitted. He finally looked at Stanley and Alex sitting across the desk from Mary and nodded. "Morning, gentlemen," he said. "What's new?"

"Well, iffen you hadn't interrupted us, we'd already know," Stanley muttered. "Mary was just getting around to letting us know what she found out, now that the idiot left."

Alex choked on his coffee, and Bradley smiled. "Which idiot?" he asked.

Clearing his throat, Alex finally choked out. "Monty Sargent."

Nodding, Bradley pulled a chair across the room to sit next to Mary and sat down. "Oh, that idiot," he replied, picking up Mary's unfinished long john and taking a bite. "Why was he here?"

"He just wanted to be sure of my credentials…" Mary began.

"He was being an ass," Stanley interrupted.

Bradley glanced at Alex questioningly.

"Stanley's right," Alex said. "He was just being an ass."

"So, did you throw him out of your office?" Bradley asked Mary.

"No, she didn't," Alex inserted. "But only because I pleaded with her behind his back."

Bradley took another bite of the long john. "You actually signed the contract?" he asked. He scratched his head for a moment and turned to Alex. "You and I didn't actually make a bet on this, did we?"

"No," Alex replied. "But I should have. I would have made good money."

Mary smiled at them both. "Now I'm the one making good money," she said. "So, let's get down to business."

"Yes, ma'am," Alex replied, and Bradley only smiled.

"Last night I had a visit from Ruth," Mary began. "First, she asked me to thank both of you for the care you took with her parents."

Alex sat upright. "She was there?"

Mary nodded. "Yes, she was able to witness how kind you were to her parents," she said, her voice filled with emotion. "It meant a great deal to her."

She took a deep breath and then continued. "But she also told me why she was out in the field that night. She was working on her senior project. She's a graduate student in Bio-engineering with an Agricultural emphasis, and she's also an intern for Granum."

"Research and development?" Alex asked.

"Yes," Mary said. "She worked in the labs. That's where she discovered that the chemicals they are spraying on the seeds are not water soluble. And they have a lifespan that carries on through the plant,

120

the fruit and the animals who are fed the tainted corn."

Alex sat back and whistled slowly. "Well, that could have opened a whole can of worms," he said. "Did she tell them?"

"She told me that she reported her information to her supervisor, who basically disregarded her comments and told her the seeds had already been tested and she was mistaken," Mary explained. "That's when she decided to turn it into a senior project and try to get it published."

"That there could be a whole lot of reasons someone might want to see her dead," Stanley said. "But that don't mean they done it."

"Well, there's a little more information that might point in that direction," Mary added. "The night she was shot, she was carrying a backpack that contained all of her research and information. She didn't like leaving it anywhere, so she always had it with her."

Alex turned to Bradley. "We didn't find a backpack with the body, did we?"

Bradley shook his head. "No, we didn't," he said. "And we didn't find a backpack with six officers searching twelve acres last night. So, I'm officially ruling out an animal dragging it away from the body."

Alex templed his hands over his chin and sat quietly for a moment. "So," he finally said. "What exactly do we know?"

"We know whoever murdered her had an agriculture background," Stanley inserted.

Mary turned to him. "How do we know that?" she asked.

"Simple. Once those farmers harvest their fields ain't no one going to be checking them until spring," he explained. "That's why her body was left where it fell. The murderer knew no hunter would be walking that close to a major highway or a cemetery, so it would not be discovered until spring."

"That was brilliant, Stanley," Alex said.

Stanley nodded. "That's why I'm Mary's assistant," he stated.

Bradley turned to Mary and whispered. "He's your assistant?"

She smiled and nodded. "I'll tell you more later," she whispered back.

Bradley chuckled softly. "I can't wait."

"Okay, we need to start the interview process," Alex said. "I pulled the articles that ran when she came up missing…"

"What happened to her car?" Mary interrupted.

"What?" Alex asked.

"Her car," Mary said. "If the murderer felt safe leaving her body in the field, as Stanley said, wouldn't they be concerned that if her car was parked close by, the officials would search the fields for her body?"

"The articles seemed to imply she was a runaway, not a victim," Alex said. "They found her car parked at the Convention and Visitors Bureau parking lot, and the sheriff's department considered it the place she was picked up."

"Why would they assume she'd just run away?" Mary asked.

"Good question," Alex said. "So, we should start with the same people the sheriff's department interviewed, her roommate, her best friend, her university advisor and her parents."

Mary nodded. "And let's add the people she worked with during her internship," she said. "It would be interesting to know who, if anyone, she told about her research project."

Chapter Twenty-four

Bradley's cruiser pulled into the parking lot of Granum. The huge four-story industrial building stretched over several acres, holding not only research and development but also inventory and transportation facilities. The outside of the building was sided in a dark gray, smooth material, and behind the main facilities, giant silos loomed overhead.

"Pretty impressive," Mary said as they walked toward the front entrance.

"Yeah, I think that's the idea," Bradley replied.

"Did you call ahead?" she asked quietly as he held open the door for her.

He smiled down and shook his head, his eyes twinkling. "Nah, I figured we'd surprise them."

They walked through the three story lobby with impressive murals of farm fields on the walls and stopped at the receptionist desk. Behind the desk, the young woman manning the phone froze when she saw Bradley.

"Good morning," he said, unsmiling. He took out his identification and showed it to her. "We need to speak with…" he glanced down at the pad he was carrying, "Darren Lorne, in research and development."

The young woman nodded. "I'll just call…" she started to reach for the phone, and Bradley placed his hand over hers and shook his head.

"There's no reason to call," he said. "If you will just give us directions, we will introduce ourselves."

"Oh," she stammered. "But I…"

"Are you trying to obstruct justice?" Bradley asked, his tone dark.

Nearly jumping away from the desk, the young woman shook her head. "Oh, no, I'm not, sir," she replied. "I'm so sorry. I'll buzz you in right away. Just take the elevator to the third floor, turn left and go to the end of the hall. You'll see the R&D labs. He's in the office just inside the door."

"Thank you," Bradley replied. "Your cooperation will be noted."

Mary and Bradley walked in silence through the heavy security doors and didn't speak until they were standing alone in front of the elevators.

"That was mean," Mary whispered. "You scared that young woman to death."

Bradley nodded. "Yeah, I almost felt sorry for her," he replied. "She must be new, or she would have called Human Resources immediately."

"Yeah, how much time do you think we have?" Mary asked, glancing over her shoulder.

"If we're lucky, we'll make it to Lorne's office just before they do," he said with a grin.

The elevator door opened, and Bradley hit the button for the third floor. With swift efficiency, the elevator brought them quickly up to the third floor, and wasting no time, they hurried towards the lab.

True to the receptionist's word, they found a nameplate with Lorne's name just inside the door next to a glass wall. Inside the office, a middle-aged man wearing a white lab coat that did not hide his paunch was drinking coffee and reviewing a report. Bradley stepped forward and knocked forcefully on the door.

Coffee sloshed dangerously as Darren Lorne quickly glanced over his shoulder and then did a double take when he saw Bradley's uniform. Placing the coffee cup on a pile of papers, he pushed himself to his feet and hurried to the door.

"Is there a problem here?" he asked, looking around. "Are we being evacuated?"

Bradley shook his head slowly and then met Darren's eyes for a long moment. "I need to ask you some questions," he said. "May we sit down?"

Darren swallowed audibly. "Am I under suspicion for something?" he asked.

"Not at this point," Bradley replied. "We're just asking some preliminary questions in an investigation."

Darren nodded. "Sure, come in," he said, moving a stack of papers from a chair and offering it to Mary, then doing the same for Bradley.

Once he had taken his seat, Bradley leaned forward. "I'd like to ask you about Ruth McCredie," he said, watching the man's reaction carefully.

Darren seemed to relax in his chair. He casually picked up his coffee cup and sipped. "Oh, Ruth," he said. "Yeah, great girl. Smart girl." He shrugged. "I don't know much about her. She just up and left town. Didn't even ask for a reference."

"Would you have given her a reference?" Mary asked.

"Oh, yeah, sure," he said. "I mean, I don't think it's a good practice to leave halfway through an internship, but that girl has smarts. Real smarts. And, you know, she's young. They do stupid things sometimes."

"Mr. Lorne, did you watch the news last night?" Bradley asked.

Darren shook his head. "No, I worked late and then caught the last few minutes of the game before I went to bed. Why?"

"Ruth McCredie's body was found yesterday," Bradley replied. "In a field. Not too far from this building. She was murdered."

Chapter Twenty-five

The coffee cup slipped with a crash to the ground, and Darren stared wide-eyed at Bradley and Mary. "Mu-mu-murdered?" he stammered, his hand shaking.

Bradley nodded.

"Oh that poor girl," he said, shaking his head. "Oh, her poor parents." Then he looked at Bradley. "Who did it?"

"Well, Mr. Lorne, we don't know yet," Bradley replied. "And that's why we're here."

Darren's eyes widened and he sat back in his chair. "You don't think that I…"

"We are not making any accusations at this point," Bradley said. "But we would appreciate your full cooperation."

"Of course," he said, grabbing hold of the edge of his desk to calm his shaking hands. "What can I do?"

"Well, Mr. Lorne, was there anyone here that had any troubles with Ruth?" Mary asked.

Darren shook his head. "No, nothing at all like that," he replied. "She was just down-to-earth and hardworking."

"We'd like to interview the other people she worked with," Bradley said. "Could you…"

At that moment, the door to Darren's office opened and a trim, professionally coiffed, woman in a navy blue suit stepped inside. "Excuse me," she said tersely. "But I need to end this interrogation with our employee."

Bradley turned in his seat and stood up. "This is not an interrogation, Ms…" he paused and waited.

"Tate. Angela Tate," she replied. "I'm the Regional Vice President of Granum, and the proper protocol would have been to come to my office first and request permission to speak with one of our employees."

"Well, Ms. Tate," Bradley replied. "When it comes to a murder investigation, I'm not overly concerned about what your protocol is. I just want to solve a crime."

Score! Mary cheered silently.

"However, if you would prefer that I send several of my units here to pick up the folks in your company I wish to interview, as well as yourself," he continued, "I'd be happy to oblige. I just thought it would be less…public if I came here myself."

Double score! Mary thought.

"And your companion?" Ms. Tate asked haughtily, quickly glancing in Mary's direction and then looking away.

Mary stood, glad she'd changed into a business outfit and extended her hand. "I'm Mary O'Reilly," she said, thinking it would be wise to leave off her new last name. "I'm a consultant with the District Attorney's Office on the case. But I agree with Chief Alden. If you would rather meet with us at either the Police Department or the Court House, I'm sure we could arrange it."

Angela Tate took a deep breath and pasted on a smile. Mary could tell she hated losing.

"Why, of course we mean to cooperate with the authorities in any way we can," she said. "What can we do to help you with your investigation?"

"If you or Mr. Lorne could show us where Ruth worked," Mary said, "that would be a good start. And, if there were any items she left behind before she disappeared, those would be helpful, too."

"We'd also like access to her files at her work station," Bradley added.

"I'm afraid those files belong to the company and are confidential," Angela stated.

Mary shrugged. "We can get a warrant," she said easily. "It's not a problem."

Angela inhaled sharply. "That won't be necessary," she said, and Mary was sure she saw her clench her jaw. "We will be happy to cooperate. Please, come this way."

She opened the office door and motioned to Darren. "Darren, why don't you lead this little tour," she offered.

As soon as they walked into the lab room, Mary's attention was drawn to the number of white rat ghosts that clambered all over the pristine steel tables and white shelves. Casually, she put her hand on Bradley's arm and bit back a laugh when his eyes widened in horror.

"Do you do a lot of experimenting with lab rats?" Mary asked, looking around the room to locate the cages.

A telling look flew between Angela and Darren, and then Angela shook her head. "No, we really try to limit our experimentation," she said. "We are PETA friendly and are a huge supporter of the ethical treatment of animals."

A large ghost rat dropped from a hanging light fixture above Angela's head and fell onto her shoulder. She involuntarily shivered, and the rat fell to the floor and scampered away. "Well, that's good to know," Mary replied. "So, you don't use any rats for testing?"

"Oh, no, I didn't say that," Angela corrected. "We just limit our use to a judicious few and only to protect our consumers."

They turned the corner to see a large work area in front of them with four work stations. "This is where our interns work," Darren explained. "Ruth's work station was the one in the corner."

The other three works stations were occupied, and Mary was surprised that many of the rats seem to be congregating around one area in particular. Several of the rats looked up and met Mary's eyes. *Oh, no*, she thought, *I do not want ghost rats following after me.* She quickly turned away from them, hoping the damage hadn't already been done.

"Chandler, may I have a moment?" Darren asked, and the student in that area turned around.

He looks like a teen heart-throb, with sun-bleached blonde hair, a tan and a well-muscled physique, Mary thought. *Even his teeth are perfect.*

"Chandler worked with Ruth on several projects," Darren said. "I'm sure he'd be able to help you with any questions you might have."

Bradley nodded. "Thank you," he replied and then he turned to Angela. "If you could provide a private space where we could…" He paused for a moment. "interview your interns, that would be very much appreciated."

"Of course," she replied coolly. "There's a conference room at the end of the hall. I'll have it cleared and set up for you. How long do you think you'll need it?"

"No longer than three hours," he said. "And what time would be good for you?"

She froze, surprised, and stared at him. "Excuse me?"

"What time would be best for us to interview you?" he asked. "I just want to be sure we have your statement on record, too."

"I will make myself available whenever you would like," she said, her smile tightening. "And now, if that's all, I'll see to the conference room."

"Thank you, Ms. Tate," Bradley said. "You've been very helpful."

"Don't mention it," she replied tersely.

The review of Ruth's computer turned up only Granum files. Even her emails were job specific. After forty-five minutes of reviewing files, Bradley shook his head. "I'll have my tech guys go over this again," he said, "in case there are some hidden or deleted files, but at this point, it looks clean."

He looked over at Darren. "I'd like one of my tech staff to take her computer to the station for further review," he said. "I'll be happy to sign a receipt stating we have it, but at this point I have to consider it as evidence."

Darren nodded. "No. No problem," he said. "I'll let them know at the front desk."

"Thank you," Bradley said. "Now if you could show us that conference room, we'll get the interviews started."

Chapter Twenty-six

Mary and Bradley seated themselves on the side of the conference table that faced the door.

"I don't think Ms. Tate was taken in by your charm," Mary teased.

"Really?" Bradley replied, smiling at her. "And here I tried my best to win her over."

"I don't think she likes to be crossed," Mary said.

Bradley's face turned serious, and he nodded. "I agree," he said. "And the next thing we need to learn about her is if she has access to a gun."

"Do you think…" Mary gasped, shocked.

Bradley shrugged. "Motive and opportunity," he said. "That's all it takes."

A knock on the door halted their discussion, and Chandler poked his head into the room. "Are you ready for me?" he asked.

Nodding, Bradley motioned him to the chair across from them. "Yes, please come in," he said.

Chandler closed the door and hurried over to the chair. He smiled at Mary and gave her a half-wink before sitting down.

"He does that to all the girls," Ruth said, appearing in the seat next to Chandler. "I told him it was a little obvious."

Mary bit back a smile and focused on Chandler. "Were you and Ruth friends?" she asked.

He shook his head in confusion. "What do you mean were?" he asked. "Ruth and I are still friends."

"He doesn't know," Ruth said and then shrugged. "He never watches the news. He only watches the cooking and home improvement shows."

"You probably missed the news," Mary said. "We found Ruth's body yesterday."

"What?" Chandler exclaimed, clearly surprised as he shook his head in denial. "No. No, Ruth is way too young to die. She was so healthy. She was always, like, drinking milk. You have to be mistaken."

"Really?" Ruth asked. "You think milk stops bullets?"

"No, it was Ruth's body," Bradley said. "Her parents confirmed it last night."

"How did she die?" he pleaded.

"She was shot," Mary replied. "She was murdered."

For a moment, Chandler went so pale that Mary thought he was going to faint. "Are you okay?" she asked.

"Wow, he's taking this hard," Ruth said softly.

The young man took a slow, deep breath and leaned forward. "Do you know why she was murdered?" he asked quietly, glancing carefully around the room.

"We have our suspicions," Bradley said. "But why don't you tell us what you think might have happened."

Chandler glanced around the room once more. "This room is clean, isn't it?" he asked.

Ruth sighed and rolled her eyes. "Okay, other than the cooking and home improvement shows, he watches a lot of spy stuff."

Mary turned to Bradley. "You know," she whispered. "They were the ones that suggested this room. We could have company."

Bradley nodded, pulled out his cell phone, clicked on an application, and suddenly the room was filled with noises.

"What's that?" Chandler asked.

"An audio jammer created by a scientist at mynoise.net," Bradley said. "It's specifically made to interrupt listening devices. Now all we have to do is keep our voices fairly low and no one will be able to hear us."

"That is seriously cool," Chandler said. "It's safe now?"

"Yes," Bradley said. "Tell us what you think."

"Well, Ruth, she was…she was almost inhuman she was so smart," he said.

"That was a weird compliment," Ruth said, screwing up her face.

"She knew this biotech stuff like the back of her hand," he continued. "So, one day I'm working on some routine stuff, and she calls me over to her workstation. She's all excited. She tells me to look into her microscope, so I do and I see these, like, squiggly things. I look up and she's smiling at me, like whatever I saw is a big deal. And I say, What?"

"He had no idea what I was talking about," Ruth inserted.

Shaking his head, Chandler wipes a few stray tears from his eyes. "Sorry. It's, you know, I just saw her smile, in my mind and I know I'm never going to see it again," he said softly.

"Awww," Ruth said and brushed a few tears of her own away. "That was totally sweet."

He took a deep breath and continued. "So, she punches me lightly and calls me a dork, but then she tells me that the bacteria in the slide is from the special seed coating Granum puts on their corn seed. It prevents a whole lot of stuff, but then it's supposed to just die off in the soil. And that squiggly thing isn't dead."

"So Granum wasn't telling the truth about their seeds?" Bradley asked.

Chandler nodded eagerly. "Right. Exactly. It was like false advertising, or worse," he said. "So Ruth said she was going to tell Darren about it. And I was like, Ruth don't you think they already know?"

He shook his head. "She came back to her desk, like an hour later, and she was really upset," he said. "Darren took her up to see the dragon...I mean Ms. Tate. And they said something about a confidentiality agreement she signed with her internship, and if she shared her findings with anyone they would sue her and her parents and they'd lose their farm."

"Did she stop?" Mary asked, already knowing the answer.

He shook his head. "No. She said these bacteria could hurt people, and she knew her parents would want her to tell the truth," he said, and then he looked up at Mary and Bradley. "But I don't think her parents would have wanted her dead."

Ruth stared at him for a long moment and then slowly shook her head. "No," she said as she started to fade away. "No they wouldn't have."

Chapter Twenty-seven

The next intern was the only other woman on the team, Sonja Morgan. She was tall and thin with bright red hair and a scattering of freckles across the bridge of her nose. Mary smiled when she walked through the door. "Sonja, thank you for meeting with us," she said.

"I didn't think I had a choice," Sonja replied.

Bradley met her eyes and nodded. "You're correct, you didn't," he replied. "Ms. O'Reilly was just being polite."

Sonja rolled her eyes and settled in the chair. "So?" she asked.

"So, I see by your records that you're older than the other students in the intern program," Mary said.

"Is my age relevant to your investigation?" she asked.

"At this point, we don't know what's relevant or not," Bradley said. "So, we'd appreciate your cooperation."

With an impatient sigh, Sonja turned to Mary. "Unlike my fellow interns, I had to pay my own way through school," she said. "So, I've had to skip semesters and work to earn enough money. That's why I'm older."

"How well did you know Ruth?" Bradley asked.

"We were roommates," Sonja said. "We shared an apartment in Freeport near the community college."

"Were you interviewed when she disappeared?" Mary asked.

"No, because I was the one who called the police," Sonja replied. "Ruth was out late sometimes, but never overnight. When I woke up the next morning and saw that she hadn't come home, I called 911."

"What did you think happened to her?" Mary asked.

Sonja glared at Mary for a moment, her angry eyes filling with tears. "I thought she was dead," she spit out. "I thought she had finally gone too far and someone had killed her. I thought we were all going to die just because Miss Smarty-pants couldn't keep her nose out of someone else's business."

"Whose business?" Bradley asked.

Sonja turned to him. "You just interviewed Prince Charming, so you know all about Ruth's project and the seeds," she said. "She spent night after night in the labs at the community college running tests. And you could see from that stupid smile on her face, she'd found her evidence."

"Did you warn her?" Bradley asked.

"Hell, yeah," she said. "She was such an idealist. She was so sure people would be pleased with her findings." Sonja buried her face in her hands for a moment. Finally, she looked up and the anger was gone, replaced with sadness. "She was nice to me. She lent me money, she helped me with homework. She helped me get a scholarship for next semester. Why the hell was she so damn stupid?"

"I know it sounds like we're asking the same questions," Mary said. "But we need to be sure we are hearing what you're saying. Do you think someone from Granum was responsible for Ruth's death?"

Sonja took a deep breath and glanced around the room. "Yeah," she said. "It might not have been someone from this office that actually pulled the trigger, but they were the ones who had the most to lose. They were the ones who Ruth was going to threaten." She shook her head with certainty. "Yeah, it was someone from Granum alright."

Chapter Twenty-eight

Charlie Paul was everything Chandler was not. His thick glasses perched on the end of his thin, long nose, and his dark hair was oily and unkempt, like he often forgot to wash it. His complexion was pallid and scattered with acne. He had a slight build, wore dark, loose clothing, and was only about five feet tall. He kind of reminded Mary of a Goth scarecrow.

"Charlie, thank you for meeting with us," Mary said.

Charlie slipped meekly into the chair and nodded. "My pleasure, ma'am," he replied.

"How well did you know Ruth?" Bradley asked him.

Charlie pushed up his glasses and stared owlishly at Bradley. "We worked together as interns," he said.

"Other than your work?" Bradley asked.

Charlie shrugged. "She was from the University of Illinois, I was from Wisconsin," he said. "So we really didn't know each other more than here."

"Did you hear about her death?" Bradley asked.

Charlie nodded. "Yeah, I heard about it on the news last night," he said.

"But you didn't tell anyone here at Granum," Bradley said.

"I didn't want to be that guy," he replied.

"That guy?" Bradley asked.

"You know, that guy who gives people bad news," he replied with a shrug. "So, I just wanted to wait until someone else brought it up."

"Did you socialize with her?" Mary asked.

"Socialize?" he repeated, confused.

"Did you go out and have drinks or pizza with her?" Bradley asked. "See her outside of work?"

"Like date her?" Charlie asked, pushing the glasses up again. "You asking me if I dated her?"

Mary shook her head. "No, we just wanted to know if you ever saw her, with the group, outside of this building."

Charlie stared at Mary for a long moment. "A couple times we all drove back into Freeport for lunch," he said. "I saw her then."

"Did you work on any projects together?" Mary asked. "Here at Granum?"

He shook his head. "Naw, she didn't like how I did my experiments," he said. "So, we never worked together."

Charlie's words reminded Mary of something she'd seen at the work stations. "You mentioned that she didn't like how you did your experiments," she said. "Can you tell me if Chandler uses a lot of rats for his experiments."

A slow smile crossed Charlie's face. "That's the big joke here," he said. "Chandler really likes the rats." He chuckled shyly. "Yeah, he really likes those rats."

"But Ruth didn't like the rats?" Bradley asked.

"Ruth didn't have time for those kind of experiments," he said. "She was working on her special project." He pushed his glasses up again. "I mean, don't get me wrong, Ruth would always get her work done. But then she'd work on her project. She said she didn't have time for games."

"Do you and Chandler have time for games?" Mary asked.

Charlie shrugged. "Not too often," he said. "Mostly we just do the experiments and note the results."

148

"Do you have any thoughts about who might have killed Ruth?" Bradley asked.

Charlie thought about it for a moment and then shook his head. "Someone who wanted her dead, I guess," he said.

"And do you know who would have wanted her dead?" Bradley asked.

"Well, I think that report she was writing could have gotten a lot of attention," he said. "So, you know, maybe someone didn't want Ruth to get all that attention."

"Do you think someone at Granum could have killed her?" Mary asked.

Charlie looked slowly around the room and then pushed his glasses up once more. "Well, really, who else is there?"

Chapter Twenty-nine

Mary sat back and sighed after Charlie left the room. "Well, we have a lot of witnesses for motive," Mary said.

Bradley nodded and picked up his phone to quickly glance at his emails. "Yeah, and not a whole lot of anything else," he replied. "Are you hungry?"

She smiled. "Starved. And I really have to go to the bathroom," she said.

"Well, I noticed the bathroom is down the hall and around the corner," he said. "And I just sent a text to Alex to have him come join us when we interview Angela Tate and Darren. I think we need to bring in the big guns for this interview."

She nodded. "That's a good idea," she said.

"And I told him to pick up lunch and bring it with him."

She smiled widely. "And that's a great idea."

He chuckled. "Okay, go use the bathroom, and then we can go over our notes until Alex gets here."

Slipping from the conference room, Mary made her way into the women's room and a stall at the far corner of the room. A little while after she'd locked the stall door, Mary heard the door to the bathroom open.

"What did they ask?" the now familiar tone of Angela Tate's voice echoed in the small, tiled room.

"I don't know," Sonja answered. "Just the usual questions you get during a murder investigation."

"Don't be a smart-ass," Angela snapped. "Don't forget. Without me you wouldn't have this internship."

Mary listened intently and heard Sonja's sigh. "You know, I don't think that would be a really wise move on your part," Sonja replied easily. "Admitting that you brought someone in to spy on the rest of the interns might make you look, I don't know, suspicious."

Mary really wished she could see Angela's face. Then she smiled, quickly finished in the stall and flushed the toilet. She exited the stall and turned to the surprised women standing in the middle of the bathroom.

"Well this is awkward," Mary said with a little grimace as she walked over to the sinks to wash her hands. "Although, really, it will make our interview with you, Ms. Tate, so much more interesting."

The other two women still stood in shock while Mary pulled a paper towel out of the dispenser, quickly dried her hands, tossed it into the waste receptacle and shrugged at both of them before exiting the bathroom. She allowed a smile to grow on her face as she walked back down the hall towards the conference room.

"Sonja was spying on me?" Ruth asked, appearing next to Mary.

"So, you heard that?" Mary whispered.

"Yeah, I heard it," Ruth said. "Sonja was my roommate. I thought she was my friend. How could she spy on me?"

Mary hurried into the conference room and closed the door. Ruth glided through the door behind her.

"Mary," Bradley began, but Mary held her hand up to stop him.

"Ruth's here," she said, before turning her attention to the ghost. "You don't know what circumstances caused Sonja to agree to spy for Angela."

Bradley's eyebrows raised, and Mary nodded. "I know, right?" she said to him.

Turning back to Ruth, she continued. "I've learned that until I have all the evidence, I shouldn't jump to conclusions," Mary said. "Sonja could have been true to your friendship. She could have kept your secrets. We don't know yet."

Ruth sighed. "Okay, you're right," she said. "But it still sucks."

Mary nodded. "Yeah, it really does suck," she agreed. "But don't condemn Sonja until we get all the information."

A knock on the conference door interrupted their conversation. Mary opened the door to find Sonja there. "Can I talk to you?" she asked.

Mary opened the door wider and motioned her inside.

"I don't know how much you overheard…" she began.

"Pretty much everything," Mary inserted.

Sonja sighed. "Okay, so here's the deal," she said. "Angela is my stepmom."

"I didn't know that," Ruth exclaimed.

"I didn't have a lot of choice about being a spy," Sonja continued. "If I wanted the internship, I had to agree to watching out for Angela's best interests."

"How much did you tell her about Ruth's project?" Mary asked.

"Not much," she said. "I mean, she already knew what Ruth had found out because Ruth told Darren and then they both spoke with Angela. So, Angela would ask about it, but I'd just tell her that she scared Ruth with the threat against her parents."

She paused for a moment, and her eyes glistened. "Listen, Ruth was one of the few people I ever met who didn't want something from me," she said. "She was a real friend. I kept warning her, because I know what my stepmother's like. I kept telling her to stop, but she wouldn't listen to me."

Mary nodded and looked over at Bradley.

"I just have one question for you," Bradley said.

"Okay," Sonja replied.

"At the end of our conversation, you said that you thought someone from Granum did this to Ruth," he said, reading from his notes. "You said they might not have pulled the trigger, but they would have hired someone to do it. Do you have any proof that Angela Tate hired someone to kill Ruth?"

Sonja shook her head. "No, I don't," she admitted. "And if I did, I would hand it over right away."

"Then why did you say that?" Mary asked.

"Because she's a cold-hearted bitch," Sonja replied. "And I think she's capable of anything when it comes to her job and this company."

Chapter Thirty

A few minutes after Sonja left the conference room Bradley's phone rang. "It's Alex," he said to Mary before picking it up.

"Hey, what's up?" he asked without preamble. He paused, listened and sighed. "Yeah, well that makes a whole lot of sense considering what Mary just overheard." He paused again. "Sure, we can be there in about ten minutes."

He hung up the phone and turned to Mary. "Granum has officially lawyered up," Bradley said. "They want to postpone our interviews with Angela and Darren until they can have their lawyers present."

Mary shook her head. "You know, I realize that I just told Ruth she shouldn't jump to any conclusions until she has all the facts," she said. "But Angela Tate…"

Bradley nodded. "Yeah, sometimes you aren't jumping, you're being pushed. So, Alex wants us to meet him at Imperial Palace for lunch. Is that okay with you?"

"That sounds great," she replied, her stomach echoing her statement. "I think Mikey wants Chinese food."

Bradley held the conference door open for her. Mary walked out into the hallway and then stopped. "I'd really like to go back into the lab one more time before we leave," she said. "If that's possible."

Bradley smiled at her, then patted his uniform pocket. "I must have dropped my pen somewhere," he said to Mary. "Have you seen it?"

She smiled back. "I'm sure the last time I saw you with it was in the lab," she replied. "I'm sure you were taking notes."

He sighed. "Well, then, I guess we'll just have to go back to the lab and look."

They walked down the hall, away from the elevator and back towards the lab. Pushing open the door, they entered and saw Darren and Angela in an animated conversation in Darren's office. The conversation came to an abrupt halt when Angela noticed them. She hurried to the office door.

"I'm sorry, but perhaps you haven't received the call from our lawyers," she said, her face brittle. "We won't be speaking with you today."

Bradley nodded. "No, we received the call," he said. "And we were on our way out when I realized I must have left my pen in the area by the interns. I'll just pick it up, and then we'll be off."

"If you don't mind," Angela said, "I'll accompany you."

"Be our guest," Mary replied with an easy smile.

The walked around the corner towards the work stations and were surprised when a side door opened and Chandler walked out, blood smeared all over his plastic gloved hands, a satisfied smile on his face. He wasn't aware of the others as he made his way back to his work station. Mary noted that he had another ghost rat on his shoulder.

"Chandler," Angela exclaimed.

Chandler froze, looked up and swallowed nervously. He whipped his hands behind his back and shook his head. "I'm sorry," he said. "I was just…just finishing up on an experiment."

"Is everything okay?" Bradley asked.

Chandler nodded. "Yeah, it is now," he said.

Bradley glanced over at Mary and she nodded stealthily, so no one else noticed. The pen quietly dropped from its concealment in Bradley's hands to the floor.

"Is that your pen?" Mary asked, pointing to it on the floor.

Bradley bent, picked it up and examined it. "Sure is," he replied. He turned to Angela. "Thank you for your cooperation. I'm sure we'll be seeing you soon."

Bradley and Mary turned and walked back through the lab.

"I wonder what she's going to say after we leave," Bradley whispered.

"She's not very good at waiting for the right time and the right place," Mary replied softly. "Should we see if we get lucky?"

They both paused for a moment just after they turned the corner. Mary held onto a table, pretending she was adjusting her shoe. Moments later they heard Angela's voice chastising Chandler. "What do you think you're doing?" she asked. "I specifically ordered no more animal experiments today."

"I didn't think anyone would see me," Chandler admitted. "I thought it would be safe."

"You need to stay away from those rats, Chandler," she said. "I'm getting tired of warning you."

"Yes, ma'am," Chandler replied, his voice apologetic. "I'll try."

Chapter Thirty-one

Mary and Bradley walked in silence until they were inside the cruiser, seat-belted and driving away from the facility. "I don't know about you," Mary said. "But that last incident with Chandler raised him on my creepy suspect list."

"What do you think he was doing?" Bradley asked.

"Well, whatever it was, the rat lost," Mary replied. "He was wearing another rat ghost on his shoulder when he walked out of the room."

Bradley turned off Highway 20 and onto South Street towards Imperial Palace. "I remember back when I was studying criminal justice that cruelty to animals in children was a forewarning of other criminal behavior," he said, and then he continued. "And it's also a sign of someone who was abused."

"Well, he's not a child any longer, and it seems like this might be a problem. His work station was covered with rat ghosts," Mary said. "Much more than any of the other interns. So, it must mean something."

Bradley pondered Mary's words for a few moments. "But his behavior during the questioning,"

Bradley said. "He looked genuinely surprised when we told him about Ruth's death. And distraught."

"You're right," she said. "He was on my least likely list. But, sociopaths can look you straight in the eye and lie. I'm not saying he's a sociopath, but there are plenty of believable liars out there."

Bradley turned down IHM Boulevard and into the parking lot for Imperial Palace Restaurant. "Well, it will be interesting to get Alex's take on all this," he said. "A different perspective."

"I agree," Mary replied. "Now let's get inside. I'm starving."

After they placed their orders, they shared the results of their visit to Granum.

"Everything seems to point to Granum," Alex said. "But is this just too easy? Are we missing something?"

Picking up a crab Rangoon, Mary broke a piece off and nibbled on it before answering. "I think what separates this from just a random shooting or from another motive is the disappearance of the backpack with the information about the seeds," Mary said. "Ruth was not very good at keeping a secret from her fellow interns, so would those conversations have been overheard? It sounds like her findings could have put Granum in financial risk."

Alex nodded. "Okay, let's go with that premise," he said. "Her report, if finished and published, could have devastated Granum. There are a lot of other ways to bury information like that. The confidentiality clause you mentioned. They could have made good on their threat of a law suit. They could have paid her off. It happens all the time. There are so many other options than cold-blooded murder. Why do it? Why take the risk?"

"What if Granum didn't know about the problem with its seeds?" Bradley asked. "What if the secret isn't a Granum secret, but a Darren and Angela secret? What if they assured Granum that everything was fine, but changed the reports? What if their careers and reputations were on the line?"

"That makes cold-blooded murder a more reasonable, if you'll forgive my choice of words, option," Mary said. "Angela or Darren or both don't have the financial resources of Granum. They could only bluff, and when they saw Ruth wasn't caving to their bluff, they had to get rid of the problem."

"Okay. Yes, that's a viable scenario," Alex said. "But would they call in a corporate lawyer if they wanted to hide the secret?"

Mary shrugged. "I guess it all depends on if the lawyer is in on it or not," she said.

"Good point," Alex replied.

Their food was served, and they waited until the server left before they continued their conversation. "So," Alex said, while picking up a water chestnut with his chopsticks. "Why would any of the interns be involved?"

Mary stabbed a piece of sweet and sour chicken with her fork and shook her head. "I really don't know if they are," she said. "They all admitted to knowing about Ruth and her special project. They all seemed to like and admire her. What's their motive?"

"Good question," Bradley replied. "But what if the disappearance of the backpack was intentionally done to throw us off track? If they all knew, they all would know we would be looking in that direction."

Mary froze, her fork halfway to her mouth, and turned to Bradley. "Crap. You could be right," she said. "They were all at Granum because they were smart. Smart enough to steer the focus of an investigation in a totally different direction?"

Alex picked up a piece of steamed chicken. "So, this conversation has widened the field rather than narrowed it," he said. "And what other leads haven't we followed?"

"Well, Sonja mentioned that Ruth used the labs at the community college to do her research,"

Mary said. "So, I thought if you could get me access, Alex, I'd check those out tonight."

"Mary, I can do that," Bradley offered. "I don't like the idea of you going alone."

She smiled at him. "First, thank you," she said. "But if Ruth appears, you're not going to be able to see her or get any information. And second, you need a good night's sleep. But I have a solution. I can take my new assistant."

"Stanley?" Alex asked with a smile.

"Exactly," Mary replied.

Chapter Thirty-two

"Dadgummit, why you decided to get involved with this tomfoolery I'll never know," Stanley grumbled as they walked across the dark parking lot towards the Agricultural Science building.

Mary stopped in her tracks and turned to Stanley. "Are you serious?" she asked.

"As a long-tailed cat in a rocking chair factory," he replied.

"This was your idea," she exclaimed. "You were the one who told me to take on this job."

"Yeah, well, that was afore I knew I'd be wandering around dark parking lots in the middle of the night," he said, glancing over his shoulder.

"Stanley, come off it," Mary said, placing her hands on her hips. "What gives? You, of all people, are not nervous about walking around at night."

He studied her for a moment as he rubbed his chin thoughtfully. "Iffen I tell you, you'll stay calm?" he asked.

She took a deep breath and held it for a moment. "Stanley, I'm cold, pregnant, and I have to go to the bathroom, again," she replied. "My hormones are messing with my emotional stability. I can't sleep at night and I am right now, at this very moment, craving another Crab Rangoon. So, I'm not promising anything, okay?"

His eyes widened slightly, and he took one small step away from her. "You're getting a might ornery, Mary," he replied. "But I reckon it's better I tell you now." He paused for another moment.

"Stanley, please remember the 'I have to go to the bathroom' part," she urged.

"Okay. Okay. I just don't have a good feeling about this," he said. "I ain't one to put much stock in intuition, but this just don't smell right."

She nodded. "I agree with you," she said simply. "Now, let's go inside."

She started forward towards the dark building while Stanley stood frozen and surprised, watching her go. Finally, with a shake of his head, he hurried forward to catch up. "You agree?" he asked her as they moved together towards the building.

"Uh-huh," she replied.

"Then why are we doing this?" he asked.

She sighed, glanced over at him for a moment, and then kept walking. "Because the reason you're feeling like there's something in there, is because there's something in there." She shrugged. "And we need to find out just what it is."

166

He paused for a moment, trying to figure out her logic, and then Stanley nodded. "Well, o' course we do," he said gently. "We have to find out."

"Thank you, Stanley," she said.

"Don't worry, girlie," he replied. "With me by your side, ain't nothing going to happen to you or little Mikey."

"That's what Bradley said," she said, continuing to walk towards the entrance.

"What?" Stanley asked, surprised.

She looked over her shoulder at the old man. "Bradley said he was sure I would be safe because you would be with me," she replied, pleased at seeing the smile wash across Stanley's face. "He knew you would protect me."

Stanley inhaled sharply, puffing his chest out slightly, and nodded with confidence. "Well, o' course he'd say that. He knows there's a warrior inside this body. I may look a little older, but I still got it."

Mary bit back a smile and nodded. "I believe that was nearly exactly what Bradley said, too," she said, pulling the key out of her pocket and putting it into the lock.

Stanley grinned. "Well, what are we waiting for?" he asked. "We got a case to solve."

Mary laughed. "Why, yes. Yes, we do."

Chapter Thirty-three

The Science and Agriculture Building was built in the 1970s, and the architect tried to duplicate the popular Prairie Style made famous by Illinois architect Frank Lloyd Wright. But unfortunately, although the outside had clean lines and a modern look, the sprawling inside was dark and closed in, even on the sunniest days. Tonight, even with the emergency lights placed every ten feet in the center of the ceilings, the halls were filled with shadows that made Mary feel a little more than anxious. The dim fluorescent lights didn't even reach the walls on either side.

"I shoulda brought a flashlight," Stanley muttered, staying close to Mary's side.

She nodded. "I thought since we were investigating inside we wouldn't need one," she said.

A movement at the far end of the hall had them both scurrying into the shadows against the wall and waiting. "Are you okay?" Stanley whispered.

"I have to pee," Mary admitted, her voice strained.

"Well, not to be unsympathetic," Stanley whispered back, "but your dadgum pee is going to have to wait."

They slowly moved forward, hugging the wall for concealment, to get closer to whomever or whatever moved. A shadow danced ahead and they froze. "Looks like a ghost," Stanley whispered.

Mary glanced over her shoulder at him. "Ghosts don't cast shadows," she replied.

"They do in the movies," he countered softly.

"And elephants fly in the movies," she said.

"You telling me Dumbo ain't real?" he asked, a twinkle in his eye.

"Stanley, this is serious business," she said, trying not to grin. "Stop it."

"You still got to pee?" he asked.

"More than ever," she said.

"Hand me your phone," he requested.

She dug her phone out of her pocket and handed it to him. A moment later the flashlight on her phone had been switched on, and Stanley was pointing it up the hall. "Police," he called out. "Freeze or we're gonna shoot you dead."

"Don't shoot, please," a strangled voice cried out from just ahead of them. "I'm not armed or anything."

"Charlie?" Mary called out. "Charlie Paul?"

170

"How did you know my name?" he replied.

Mary and Stanley quickly moved forward and confronted the young man who was plastered into a corner. "What are you doing here?" Mary asked. "You go to school in Wisconsin."

Charlie turned towards them and swallowed, trying to look past the flashlight beam in his eyes. "Ms. O'Reilly?" he asked tentatively.

"That's right," Stanley growled. "And her bodyguard."

Mary bit back her laugh and took a deep breath. "Please answer the question, Charlie," she encouraged.

"Sometimes, when Ruth was working on her project," he said, "I'd come by and, you know, bring her some food or something. She was nice to me." He shrugged. "Not many people are nice to me. So…"

"So?" Stanley prompted.

"So, I wanted to come back here and say goodbye," he said quietly. "This was kind of our place, but not really. I wanted it to be our place. She just wanted me to be her friend."

"How did you get in here?" Mary asked.

He shrugged. "The doors are open until six," he said. "I just kind of waited around in the men's room until after six. Then I went to the lab."

171

"Can you show me the area she used?" Mary asked.

He nodded. "Yeah, I can do that," he said. "It's down this way."

"Wait," Stanley interrupted. "Before you do that, why don't you show us the bathroom you hid out in. Just so we can corroborate your story."

Charlie nodded nervously. "Yeah. Of course," he replied, changing direction. "It's down here."

Allowing Charlie to get a few steps before them, Mary turned to Stanley. "Why did you do that?" she asked.

"Cause where there's a men's bathroom, there's gonna be a ladies' bathroom," he said. "Folks don't think clear when they gotta pee. And I want you clearheaded."

Mary grinned. "Thank you, Stanley. That was very thoughtful."

Chapter Thirty-four

As Mary walked to the sink to wash her hands, she happened to glance into the mirror and jumped when she saw Ruth's ghost standing behind her.

"Ruth," she gasped. "You scared me."

"Sorry, Mary," Ruth replied. "I'm not used to this whole ghost thing yet."

Mary smiled in sympathy. "I understand," she replied. "I'm still not entirely used to this whole seeing ghosts thing. We thought we'd check out the lab you worked on."

"But why…" she began, but the door opening caught both of their attention.

Sonja stood frozen in the bathroom doorway, staring at Mary.

"We seem to have made a habit out of meeting in bathrooms," Mary said to her.

"Uh, yeah," Sonja replied, stepping inside the room and letting the door close softly. "I guess you're wondering why I'm here."

Mary leaned against the countertop and nodded. "Yes. Yes, I am."

"Well, the reason I'm in here," she said, glancing quickly around the bathroom, "Is because I saw Charlie with some old guy in the hallway and I didn't want them to see me."

Mary nodded and waited without saying a word.

Sonja sighed. "And the reason I'm here at the Ag Building is because I wanted to see if Ruth left anything behind that Angela might want to destroy," she said.

"How do I know that you didn't want to destroy evidence you might have left behind?" Mary asked.

"Because I didn't kill Ruth," Sonja said. "And Angela did."

"Do you have proof that Angela killed Ruth?"

Sonja shook her head petulantly. "I don't need proof," she stated. "I know."

Mary shook her head. "Unfortunately, in this country, with our legal system, people can't be arrested for being a bitch," Mary said.

Sonja's lips curled into a small smile.

"But they can be arrested for breaking and entering," Mary continued.

"I didn't break and enter," Sonja disputed, holding up a key. "I have a key to get in after hours."

"That's my key," Ruth said.

"Only if your name is Ruth McCredie," Mary said to Sonja.

"How would a security guard know if I was Ruth or not?" she asked. "I'm a girl, and I'm college aged. Bingo, I can get in."

Mary folded her arms across her chest and shook her head. "Really? Did you think about what you just said to the person representing the D.A.'s office in the murder investigation for Ruth?" she asked impatiently. "That you know how to impersonate Ruth? You really want me to know that?"

Sonja's eyes opened wide. "No. That's not what I meant," she said. "She told me about her key and gave me her password in case she ever needed me to get into the system for her. I mean I never, ever impersonated Ruth."

"Except on that blind date I didn't want to go on," Ruth whispered to Mary.

"Except on that blind date Ruth didn't want to go on," Mary said.

Sonja stepped back against the wall and shook her head. "Who are you people, and how do you know that?" she asked.

Mary shrugged. "We have our ways," she said.

Ruth chuckled. "Tell her you know that she's been borrowing the neighbor's internet access," she said.

"Although, you might want to think about getting your own internet access," Mary replied, trying her best to keep a straight face. "And stop using your neighbor's."

Sonja stared at Mary while Ruth laughed loudly. "The look on her face," Ruth chortled. "It's priceless."

Suddenly, Sonja looked up, rubbed her arms and slowly glanced around the room. "She's here," she said, amazement in her voice. "Ruth is here."

She turned back to Mary. "I'm right," she said with hope in her voice. "Ruth is here."

Mary nodded and smiled at Sonja. "You're right," she replied. "Ruth is here with us."

"Does she know who killed her?" Sonja asked.

Mary took a moment to answer, then stared straight into Sonja's eyes and nodded slowly. "Yes, she does," Mary said, looking for any kind of fearful reaction.

"Then what the hell are you doing here wasting time?" Sonja exclaimed. "Go arrest them."

"I knew it couldn't be her," Ruth said. "She truly was my friend."

"Ruth doesn't know," Mary confessed. "But now I know who didn't kill her."

"I told you I didn't do it," Sonja said. Then she paused and nodded. "Like no killer ever said that, too. I get it."

She looked around the room again. "Ruth? Ruth, how are you doing?" she asked.

Ruth rolled her eyes. "I'm dead. How does she think I'm doing?" she asked Mary.

Sonja turned to Mary. "Duh. She's dead. I guess she's not doing great," she said.

Mary nodded. "That's pretty much what she said," Mary replied.

"She can talk to you?" Sonja asked. "Are you like a medium?"

"Yes, she can talk to me," Mary said. "And she told me that she knew you didn't kill her because you were truly her friend. And, no, I'm not considered a medium. I just have this special gift to see and talk with ghosts. I help them solve their issues so they can move on."

"Issues like being murdered," Sonja said.

"Exactly," Mary replied.

"Okay, I know that I wasn't very cooperative earlier," Sonja said. "But now that I know you're on Ruth's side, I'm…I'm on your side. How can I help?"

"Well, you can help me inspect Ruth's lab area," Mary suggested. "And let me know if anything seems out of place."

"Great," Sonja said. "But, can you get rid of Charlie first? I don't want him to know I'm helping you. Word might get back to Angela."

Mary nodded and walked past Sonja to the door. "No problem," she said. "Wait here."

Sonja looked nervously around the room. "But, you know, there's a ghost in here," she said.

Mary nodded. "And she's your friend Ruth," Mary said.

Sonja relaxed visibly. "Yeah, you're right."

Chapter Thirty-five

Mary walked down the hallway to where Stanley and Charlie were waiting.

"You okay?" Stanley asked her quietly. "You took so long, I was getting a little worried."

Mary nodded. "Ruth showed up," she explained. "And someone else."

"You got two ghosts in there?" Stanley asked.

Shaking her head, Mary lowered her voice even more. "One of the other interns showed up," Mary said. "She was also Ruth's roommate. She wants to help us, but she doesn't want to be seen by Charlie."

Considering her words for a moment, Stanley nodded. "So, how about if I let him show me the lab, just so he don't get suspicious, then I send him on his way?"

"That would be great," Mary said. "Do you want me to go along?"

Stanley shook his head. "No, I'm gonna use you for my excuse," he replied with a quick smile.

He looked over at Charlie, who was studying them intently, and nodded. "Ms. O'Reilly here just got a call from the police," he said. "They got some forensic guys coming over to process the lab. We figure maybe you don't want to be here when they arrive, seeing they might not understand your reasoning for being here."

"No, sir," Charlie stammered. "I mean, yes, sir."

Stanley nodded. "Ms. O'Reilly is going to meet them at the entrance on the other side of the building. So, why don't you quickly show me the lab, and then we can get you out of here while no one is the wiser."

"Yes, sir," Charlie agreed. "It's down this way."

"I'll meet you there in a few minutes," Mary said to Stanley.

Charlie moved off in a half-run. "Come on," he said. "It's not too far."

Stanley slowly followed Charlie down the hall. It was a damn shame they weren't going to be able to interrogate this young whippersnapper. Stanley was sure the kid knew more than he was telling. But, he reasoned, he was Mary's assistant, wasn't he? Didn't he have more responsibility than just walking the kid to the door? Didn't Mary and Bradley just call him a warrior?

"Hey, Charlie, wait just a minute," he called. "I got a couple of questions for you afore I let you go."

Charlie stopped in front of the lab room. "Um, I thought I was supposed to hurry," he said.

"Well, there's hurrying, and then there's hurrying," Stanley said. "Sides, considering you're one of our primary suspects, I think you'd be eager to clear your name."

Charlie swallowed audibly. "I'm a suspect?" he asked, the words coming out in a squeak.

Stanley stared into the young man's eyes. "Yep, you and them other interns," Stanley replied. "You had the most access to Ruth. Makes sense, don't it?"

Shaking his head, Charlie leaned against the wall. "No, it doesn't make sense," he said. "Well, not with most of us."

Biting back a smile of triumph, Stanley inhaled deeply. He knew he'd be able to break him down. He continued to stare at the young man, then nodded slowly. "And what do you mean by that?" he asked.

"Well, you know, Sonja was her roommate," Charlie said. "And Ruth was a lot prettier than Sonja. And Chandler paid more attention to Ruth than

Sonja. So, you know, it could have been jealousy. Don't people kill people because they're jealous?"

Stanley rubbed his hand over his chin. "Well, sometimes they do, and sometimes they don't," he said. "I ain't saying you're correct, but you got a point there."

Charlie seemed a little relieved, and the shadow of a smile washed over his face. "And then, you know, Chandler was the one who told Ruth about the field next to Gund Cemetery."

"Wait a minute, boy," Stanley replied. "What did you just say?"

"Chandler. Chandler was the one who told Ruth that the Granum seeds were planted in the field next to Gund Cemetery," he repeated.

"How did he know that?" Stanley asked.

Charlie shrugged. "He spends a lot of time there," he said. "He likes to bury stuff on the other side of the fence line."

"Bury stuff next to a cemetery?" Stanley asked. "That ain't normal. Seems like a mighty disturbing hobby."

"I'm not saying he killed Ruth," Charlie said, "because I don't know. But, you know, maybe someone should check him out."

"Yes, young man, I think you're right," Stanley said. Smiling, he patted Charlie's shoulder. "You've done a great service to the investigation. You should be proud. I'll be sure we start investigating this Chandler in a lot more detail."

"You won't tell him I told you?" Charlie asked. "If he's the killer, I wouldn't want him to come after me."

"You probably don't have to worry about it," Stanley said, puffing out his chest slightly. "I've got a lot of experience in these kinds of things. Done a lot of reading. In most cases, when someone like this Chandler fellow kills out of an emotional release, they feel remorse, and it usually gets to them. In nine out of ten cases, they end up killing themselves before they kill anyone else."

He saw that Charlie was not reassured by his words. "But don't you worry, son," Stanley said, patting him again. "Chandler will never know what you said."

"Thank you, sir," Charlie replied. "May I leave now?"

Stanley nodded. "Yeah, you can go," he said. "And be safe out there."

Chapter Thirty-six

Mary waited until both Stanley and Charlie were around the corner before she went back into the bathroom. "We just have to wait a few minutes and then we can go," Mary said.

"Why was Charlie here?" Sonja asked.

"He said he wanted to say goodbye to Ruth," Mary replied.

"That's weird," Sonja said.

"Yeah, but Charlie's weird," Ruth commented.

Mary turned to Sonja. "Ruth said that Charlie's weird," she said.

"She's got that right," Sonja agreed. "But I guess it takes all kinds."

"Speaking of weird," Mary said, "Charlie told me that Chandler has a thing for the rats."

Both Ruth and Sonja chuckled. "Yeah, that is a little weird," Sonja agreed. "But, you know, that's Chandler, and we've come to accept it."

"I saw him leave a room connected to the work station area," Mary said. "He had plastic gloves on, and they were covered with blood."

"I saw that," Sonja said. "Angela walked in on him."

Ruth gasped. "Angela saw him leave the rat room?"

Mary turned from Ruth to Sonja. "Ruth just called it the rat room and sounded a little shocked when you said Angela saw him."

Sonja nodded. "Yeah, Angela doesn't have a lot of sympathy for Chandler's little hobby, as she calls it," Sonja said. "But, you know—"

The knock on the bathroom door interrupted her.

"It's all clear out here," Stanley said. "And time's a wasting."

"Who's that?" Sonja asked.

Mary smiled. "My friend and assistant and the old guy you saw with Charlie," she said. "He escorted Charlie out of the building for us."

"Okay, cool," Sonja said. "Let's go."

"I can't go," Ruth said to Mary.

"Why not?" Mary asked.

"I can hear my mom crying," she said, her pain displayed on her face. "I need to be there. I need to go."

Mary nodded. "Yes, you go," she said. "Sonja and I can check things out."

When Sonja walked out of the bathroom behind Mary, Stanley shook his head. "You got a party in there or something?" he asked.

Mary smiled. "Something like that," she said.

"You women," Stanley said. "You can never go to the bathroom by yourselves."

Sonja grinned. "That's because there are ghosts in our bathrooms," she said.

Stanley stared at her for a moment and shook his head. "I'll never understand women."

Chuckling, they all walked down the hall together towards the lab. "What are we gonna do iffen we don't find anything in the lab?" Stanley asked.

Mary shrugged. "We'll just keep looking," she said. "We still haven't been able to interview Angela and Darren; they might be able to shed some light on things."

"Angela won't help unless she's forced," Sonja said. "She doesn't do anything that doesn't help her."

"It's a murder investigation," Stanley said. "O' course she'll help."

Sonja shook her head. "No, she's not what you call touchy-feely," she replied. "She wouldn't throw a life-preserver to a drowning person if she thought she might get her shoes wet in the process. She's pretty self-absorbed."

"No one can be that bad," Stanley said.

Sonja snorted. "The only way I got the internship is because I happened to discover the itemized list for her plastic surgery, and I told her I'd spill the beans," she said. "And I still had to promise to be her little spy."

"Why wouldn't she want anyone to know she had plastic surgery?" Mary asked. "People do that all the time."

"Well, they don't get the company to pay for it and call it sinus work," Sonja answered.

"But, often it is sinus work," Mary said. "A deviated septum might look like a nose job, but you really need to have it fixed."

Sonja grinned. "Only if her septum deviated to her ass," she laughed. "The itemized copy included liposuction, a face lift, a nose job, a boob job and a tummy tuck. She's pretty much a Frankenstein."

"And she claimed it was sinus work?" Stanley asked. "How'd she get away with that?"

"She's the boss of the head of human resources, and Granum is self-insured," Sonja said. "She gets to sign the approvals."

"Well," Mary said with a shrug, "she looks great."

Sonja laughed. "She ought to."

Once they entered the lab and accessed Ruth's account, they could tell it had been wiped clean. "Could Charlie have done this?" Sonja asked.

"Sure," Mary said with a sigh. "But Ruth's been dead for several weeks, so anyone could have done it. Even the college could have inadvertently done it when they saw she didn't have any activity on the account for weeks."

"So now what?" Sonja asked.

"Tomorrow we talk to your stepmother," Mary replied.

Chapter Thirty-seven

"So, we can't talk to Angela and Darren until Monday," Bradley's voice echoed through the hands-free system in Mary's car.

"Really? Their lawyer can't make it tomorrow?" Mary asked, more than a little disappointed.

"He's taking Wednesday off for a long Thanksgiving holiday," Bradley said. "At least that's what they told Alex. And Alex said there's nothing we can do unless we can find evidence that specifically links one of them to Ruth's death."

Mary sighed. "No, nothing so far," she said. "The lab at the college was wiped clean. Although, it was as busy as a bus station there."

"What do you mean?" Bradley asked.

"Stanley and I ran into both Charlie and Sonja inside the Ag building," she replied. "And Stanley got some interesting information from Charlie about Chandler. Chandler was the one who directed Ruth to the field next to Gund Cemetery."

"Well, that's interesting," Bradley said.

"It seems Chandler spends quite a bit of time hanging around the outskirts of the cemetery, burying things," Mary continued.

"Okay, not interesting. Downright creepy," he replied.

"Right?" Mary asked. "You know, it probably wouldn't hurt to run a check on Chandler, just to see if he's ever had any issues."

"Yeah, I'm on it," he said.

"Okay, I'll be home in a few minutes," Mary said. "Bye."

The next call she made was to her mother. "Hi, Ma," she said when the phone was answered.

"Mary," her mother replied happily. "How are you doing?"

"Much better," Mary replied. "Thanks for your great advice."

"Well, I'm glad it helped," she said. "What can I do for you?"

"I was wondering when you and Da were planning on coming tomorrow," she said. "It looks like our investigation has a hiatus until Monday."

"Well, your Da is working the evening shift tonight, so he won't be home until after midnight," her mother said. "But, knowing him, he'll still want an early start. I'd guess we'll be on the road by about eight and to your place by ten. Will that work?"

"That will be perfect," Mary said. "I've got the turkey, but I still need to shop for a few more things. Want to come?"

"Oh, darling, I love shopping with you," she said. "How's the quilt coming?"

Mary sighed. "I haven't had a chance to work on it today," she said. "Would you be willing to help me tomorrow night, once Clarissa is in bed?"

"I'd love it," her mother replied. "So, don't worry about it tonight. Get some sleep. You sound tired."

"It's been a long and eventful day," Mary agreed.

"Is there anything you want me to bring with me tomorrow?" Margaret asked.

"Could you bring the big, enamel roasting pan?" Mary asked. "I don't think I have a pan big enough for the turkey."

"Sure I can," Margaret replied. "Should I bring some of my serving dishes, too?"

"That would be great," Mary said. "I probably don't have enough of those either."

Margaret laughed. "And how about serving utensils?"

Mary groaned. "I don't think I realized how much stuff is involved in a Thanksgiving dinner. Yes, bring those, too, and anything else you think I might need. And Ma," she paused.

"Yes, darling," her mother laughed.

"Thank you," Mary said sincerely. "I don't know what I'd do without you."

"I'm sure you'd manage, but I'm happy that you don't have to," her mother replied.

"Well, I'm home," Mary said as she pulled into her driveway. "I love you, Ma. I'll see you tomorrow."

"I love you, too, Mary," her mother said. "Have a restful night. You'll have a busy day tomorrow."

Chapter Thirty-eight

Her alarm went off early the next morning. Mary turned over quickly, shutting it off before it woke Bradley. She slid from her bed and quietly padded to the bathroom to get ready for the day. The night before, she'd already laid out her clothes and left them in the bathroom so she wouldn't disturb Bradley. Fully dressed, she quietly opened the bathroom door only to see Bradley sitting up in bed.

"Going somewhere?" he asked, one eyebrow raised.

She smiled back at him. "I'm going to watch the sunrise at one of most beautiful places in Freeport," she teased. "Gund Cemetery."

"Have you been hanging around with Chandler?" he teased. He rolled out of bed and walked across the room to her. "Are you sure you still want to do this? It's about thirty-two degrees out there."

She nodded. "Yes, I want to see if I can help those women cross over," she replied. "Since I know I won't be able to get back there for a while after today, I want to give them the chance to move on before Thanksgiving."

"Do they celebrate Thanksgiving in heaven?" he asked with smile.

"Are you kidding?" Mary teased back. "They have to!"

She reached up and gave him a quick kiss. "Make sure you wake Clarissa up in time," she said. "And remind her that Grandma and Grandpa will be here when she gets home from school."

"Like I have to remind her," he said. "She's so excited. And wait until the party. She's going to be overjoyed."

"I hope so," Mary said. "I want it to be perfect for her."

He kissed her back. "It will be," he said. "Now, go and have your cemetery fun. I'll hold down the fort. And call me if you need me."

She nodded. "I will."

The sun was not quite up when she pulled down the road to Gund Cemetery. There was a slight morning fog that drifted over the ground and gave the area an ethereal feeling. She parked her car just past the sign on the gravel drive and slipped out.

She started to walk towards the back when a movement in the distance stopped her. Someone was running, just outside the far end of the cemetery fence. She hurried across the crisp grass to the

194

closest farm fence that separated the cemetery from the cornfield and tried to get a better view of the person. By the shoulder size and stance, she could see it was a man with a fairly athletic gait. She watched, trying to get some kind of clue or a look at his face. Suddenly, she noted, on a rise just above the fog, several small ghost rats were trailing after the runner.

"Chandler," Mary whispered aloud. "It had to be Chandler."

Pulling her phone from her pocket, she quickly dialed Bradley.

"Miss me already?" he asked when he answered.

"I just saw Chandler," she said.

"What?" he asked.

"I pulled up to the cemetery, and someone started running from the far end," she said. "I hurried to the side and saw a man running away from the cemetery, across the field."

"How do you know it was Chandler?" he asked.

She sighed. "There were rat ghosts following him."

He was silent for a moment. "Well, that's not going to be easy to explain in a courtroom," he finally said.

She couldn't help it. She giggled. "No. No, it's not," she finally agreed. "Do you want me to look over the fence at what he was doing, or do you want to send one of your guys?"

"Hey, Ms. Consultant for the D.A.," he answered, "I have total trust in your ability to check out a potential crime scene. But, can you get over that fence?"

She shook her head. "You can be very rude at times, Bradley Alden," she replied.

"No. What? I didn't mean anything," he insisted.

"But, yes, I can get over the fence," she said. "I know a short cut."

She went back to the car, pulled out her gloves, some plastic bags she always carried with her and her camera. Then she made the long walk to the far end of the cemetery in the cold, fall morning. As she walked, the sun came up over the tree line, and the branches and grass sparkled in the morning beams. Taking a deep breath, she paused a moment to enjoy the magic.

"It's a beautiful day, is it not?" a shy voice asked from beside her.

Mary turned to find the cholera victim who had pointed Ruth out to her standing by her side. "Yes," Mary said with a smile. "It is a beautiful day."

"You see us," the woman continued.

Mary nodded. "It's a gift," she said. "And a responsibility."

"How so?" the woman asked.

"Do you know where you are?" Mary asked.

The woman smiled sadly. "Yes, I am in a cemetery and I've been here a very long time," she replied. "I believe I've been forgotten."

"No," Mary assured her. "Not forgotten, just turned around a little."

"What do you mean?" the woman asked.

"Look around you," Mary said. "All around you and see if you can see a bright light."

The woman looked and then nodded. "I see the light," she said. "But it has always reminded me of the brightness of the lights when I had the fever. The lights hurt, so I've stayed away from it."

"Well, that makes perfect sense," Mary said. "And now I understand why you've been here so long." She paused for a moment while she gathered her thoughts. "I realize you don't know me and have no reason to trust me…"

"I have seen you here," the woman interrupted. "Helping others."

"Good," Mary said with a smile. "That helps then because I want you to trust me when I say that this light is not like the fevered lights. This light is like the sun through a window on a cold winter's day. It's like the sun on your back as you bend to smell the flowers in the springtime."

"I remember that light," the woman said with a smile.

"Then walk towards it," Mary encouraged her. "Walk towards it and see how you feel."

The woman looked over her shoulder and then back at Mary. "Thank you," she said. "I will try."

Mary watched the woman glide across the cemetery and then slowly float into the sky until she was gone. Then she turned to see the group of women she'd seen when she'd visited on Monday. They spoke quietly to each other. Then, hand in hand, they too glided across the cemetery and up into the sky.

Mary felt the warmth of their passing over, and it brought tears to her eyes. "It is a very good day," she whispered. "Welcome home."

Then she continued toward the break in the fence she'd used the other day. Turning to her left, she followed the fence line along the outside of the cemetery until she came to a small copse of trees. She could see the dirt had been freshly dug and there were footprints in the muddy soil. She took her camera out and took photos of the footprints and the ground. But as she scoured the area, she couldn't find anything that had been left behind.

She pulled out her phone again and redialed.

"Hi, is everything okay?" Bradley asked.

"Yes, I'm fine," she replied. "Actually, I'm great."

"Did you find something?" he asked.

"No. Sorry," she said. "I'm great about something else. But let's talk about Chandler right now. There are footprints, and there is a freshly dug area. I didn't think to bring a shovel and I don't think I want to be the one to discover what's down there."

"Good, I don't want you to do it either," he said. "I'll send someone down. Do you want to wait and show them the spot, or do you want to come home and I'll head over?"

"I can wait," she said, looking over at the place where the women used to stand. "It's warmed up quite a bit since I've been here."

"Okay, I'll still have them hurry," he said.

"Thanks, sweetheart," she said. "I'll see you soon."

Chapter Thirty-nine

Mary pulled up in front of her house, surprised and delighted to see her parents' car was already there. She hurried inside to greet them and was swept up into her father's arms before she could close the door.

"My little Mary-Mary," her father said, hugging her. "And how are you feeling?"

"Just great, Da," she said, placing a kiss on his cheek.

He held her away from him, his eyes glistening with emotion. "And you look like a beauty," he said. "You're glowing, you are."

"Thanks, Da," she said.

"And when is your Ma going to get her share of hugs?" Margaret asked.

Smiling, Mary turned and threw her arms around her petite mother. "Thank you for coming," Mary said. "I can't believe you're here so early."

"Ah, well, your Da was like a grumpy old bear this morning," she teased. "'Let's go early so we can beat the rush hour traffic.' So, we're out of the house by six, and who got to drive in the early morning traffic? Not your Da I can tell you. He was asleep before we passed the first toll booth."

Timothy grinned. "I always sleep when your mother's driving," he teased. "It's a defense really. She's much too aggressive for my taste."

Margaret rolled her eyes. "Well, now, he won't be needing an afternoon nap," she said. "So he can help us with the shopping."

Timothy's eyes widened in mock horror. "Not grocery shopping on the day before Thanksgiving," he pleaded. "It's nearly as bad as Christmas shopping on the day after." He looked at Bradley for help. "I'm sure there's some project young Bradley here can use some help with, isn't there, son?"

Bradley smiled. "As a matter of fact," he said, "I have a dollhouse I've been working on for Clarissa. It could use another coat of paint and some final touches."

Timothy smiled widely. "And, well, there you have it," he said, shaking his head regretfully. "I'd have loved to go shopping with you fine ladies, but duty calls."

"Duty calls my…" Margaret let the word stay unspoken and then she turned to her daughter. "So, why don't you use the bathroom, and then we can be on our way. Perhaps we can beat some of the crowds."

"How did you know I had to go to the bathroom?" she asked her mother.

"You're pregnant, aren't you?" Margaret answered with a smile.

Mary freshened up and was ready to go in a matter of minutes. "Is there anything you'd like us to get while we're out?" she asked.

"Ah, well, if you happen to see a package of those Freeport Potato Chips, I wouldn't be minding some of those," her father said. "And, if you happen to see some of that Wisconsin Aged White Cheddar, I wouldn't say no to a bite of that. Oh, and if you happen—"

"Enough," Margaret laughed. "You'd think I never fed the man. We'll find treats for you, I promise."

Timothy laughed and gave Margaret a smacking kiss on the lips. "Well, you're the only treat I'll ever need," he teased.

Mary loved that her mother still blushed.

"Oh, enough with you," Margaret said, her cheeks blazing. "We'll be back soon. See that you get that dollhouse done."

"So what's on the menu for tomorrow?" Margaret asked as they walked to Mary's car.

"Did you know that Bradley has never had corn pudding?" Mary asked, opening the door for her mother.

"What in the world?" Margaret asked as she climbed in.

Mary climbed in the other side. "It's so funny because he thinks it's going to be sweet, like chocolate pudding, and I think to him the idea of corn and pudding is disgusting."

"He's going to be so surprised," Margaret said.

"I hope so," Mary replied. "It would be awful if he really did end up hating it."

"So, other than corn pudding," Margaret said with a smile, "what else is on the list?"

Mary listed off a traditional Thanksgiving menu with all the trimmings and then added even more.

"Are you sure you want to cook all of this?" Margaret asked.

"Well, Katie and Rosie are bringing some of it," Mary said. "The big things I have to worry about are the rolls, the turkey and stuffing and, of course…"

"The corn pudding," Margaret laughed. "And just what are all of the men and children going to be doing while we cook?"

"Oh, that's the greatest thing," Mary said. "Bradley has talked to all the men, and they are taking the kids to Read Park for a Turkey Day flag football game. So, they're leaving right after the parade and won't be back until just before dinner."

"You married a good man," Margaret said.

"I married a man who would rather play football than peel potatoes," Mary countered with a smile.

"You married a smart man," Margaret laughed.

"Exactly," Mary said.

They pulled up to the grocery store, and the parking lot was already half-filled. "Well, this might take a little longer than I thought," Mary said.

"That's okay, dear," Margaret said. "We have all day."

Mary shrugged. "You're right. We do."

Chapter Forty

Several hours later, with the back of the car filled with groceries and supplies, Mary pulled into the driveway. "Well, we did it," she said to her mother.

"I just have one question," Margaret replied.

"And that is?" Mary asked with a smile.

"Are you going to have enough room in your refrigerator for everything you just bought?"

A look of panic on Mary's face instantly revealed her answer. "I didn't even think of that," Mary said. She laid her head against her steering wheel. "I'm going to have to send Bradley out for another refrigerator."

Chuckling, Margaret placed her hand on her daughter's arm. "Don't worry," she said. "The weather's cold enough that with some coolers and ice we'll be able to store some of it on your back porch."

Mary released a sigh of relief. "Thank you, Ma," she said. "You're a genius."

Her mother shook her head. "No, darling, just someone who's done the same thing many a time," she confessed. "Now, let's get your car unpacked and into the house."

In about twenty minutes, the car was empty and the cupboards were full. Mary and Margaret were sprawled out on chairs in the living room, their feet up on the coffee table, glasses of iced herb tea in their hands and Lucky purring contentedly on Margaret's lap.

"That was exhausting," Mary said.

"Aye, I always forget how much work shopping for Thanksgiving can be," Margaret replied.

Mary took a sip of the tea. "And what do we have to do tonight?" she asked.

Margaret sighed. "Ah, well, there's the dough for the Parker Rolls to rise once and then refrigerate overnight. There's the pies to bake because the turkey will be hogging the oven most of the day. There's the Waldorf Salad to make and refrigerate, and if we're feeling energetic, we could get the deviled eggs done too."

"Ma," Mary said.

"Yes, darling," her mother replied.

"We won't be feeling energetic," Mary stated.

Her mother chuckled. "Aye, I agree with you on that," she laughed. "Oh, and then we've a quilt to complete."

Mary sat up in her chair. "That's right," she said. "The quilt. But we can't begin to work on that until after Clarissa's in bed."

"Well, then, it's a good thing we didn't overdo today," her mother replied wryly. "Because we'll be having a late night."

Mary groaned. "Yeah, good thing."

The front door opened and Bradley, Clarissa and Timothy walked in.

"And look who we found at the school," Timothy said. "This big, grown-up girl. I almost didn't recognize her."

"Grandma!" Clarissa yelled, propelling herself across the room into her grandmother's arms, Lucky making a narrow escape.

Margaret hugged Clarissa. "And how's my favorite granddaughter?" she asked.

"I'm great," Clarissa replied. "More than great."

"And why are you more than great?" Margaret asked with a wide smile.

"Because tomorrow is Thanksgiving," she said. "And everyone is coming."

"Well, that's a good reason to be more than great," Margaret replied, hugging Clarissa again.

208

Sliding her feet off the coffee table, Mary sat up. "Don't I get a hug, too?" she asked with a smile.

Clarissa hurried over to hug Mary, and then she lightly patted Mary's tummy. "Hi, Mikey," she said. "I'm home."

Mary's stomach shifted, and Mary looked at Clarissa. "I think he knows your voice," she said. "He always kicks when you get home."

"He just can't wait to meet me," Clarissa said confidently.

Timothy chuckled. "Aye, he can't wait to play with his big sister."

Bradley walked across the room and gave Mary a kiss. "How was shopping?" he asked.

"Well, we left a few things on the shelves for everyone else," Mary said, "but not much."

"Great," he replied. "I'm starving. What's for dinner?"

Mary glanced at her mother, and Margaret shook her head. Then Mary looked back at Bradley. "I'm thinking pizza delivery sounds just about perfect."

Chapter Forty-one

While Clarissa and Timothy played with Lucky on the floor in the living room, Mary, Margaret and Bradley cleaned up the remainder of the pizza and started getting things started for the next day's dinner.

"Bradley, if you keep eating the slices of apple, there won't be anything left for the pie," Margaret teased as she watched her son-in-law snatch another cinnamon and sugar coated piece of apple.

"Sorry, Ma," he said, although there was a complete lack of sincerity in his voice. "These are just so delicious."

Mary tossed him the peeler. "And now you need to peel another apple," she said.

"My pleasure," he replied before snatching one more slice.

"Bradley," both women called at the same time.

Chuckling, he picked two apples out of the bag and held them up. "Two, okay?" he teased. "And I'll try to control myself."

Mary looked over her mother's shoulder and watched as she worked the lard into the pie crust.

"Someday," Mary said, "when I'm not so stressed about everything turning out perfectly, I want you to teach me how to do that."

Margaret stopped. "I can show you now," she offered.

Mary shook her head. "No, you concentrate on this crust, and I'll fill the ones you already made with pumpkin," she said.

"Don't forget to check the oven," Margaret warned her.

"Oh, that's right," Mary said. "I almost forgot."

She hurried over to the oven and pulled out a cookie sheet. "I got them just in time," Mary said. "Ma, do you have a built in timer in your head, too?"

Margaret laughed. "Sometimes I wonder if I do."

Mary brought the hot cookie sheet over to the counter to cool, and the scent of cinnamon-sugar drifted throughout the house. Bradley stopped peeling and looked up. "What's that?" he asked.

Mary turned to her mother. "What is this called?" she asked. "Officially?"

"Leftover crust with butter, sugar and cinnamon," Margaret replied with a chuckle. "Officially."

Bradley put the peeler down on the table and walked over to the counter. "It looks amazing," he said, scooping up a piece of the flat, flaky crust. "Ouch, it's hot."

Mary grinned. "Really?" she teased. "Because I just pulled it out of the oven. I don't know why it would be hot."

"Smart aleck," Bradley replied, and after tossing the hot pastry between his hands, he quickly popped it in his mouth.

"Ah…ah…ah!" he said, open mouthed as he chewed down. "I don't know why I thought putting it in my mouth would be a good idea."

"How does it taste?" Mary asked.

"Aside from the third degree burns," he said, "delicious."

Clarissa and Timothy came in from the living room. "Can I try some?" Clarissa asked.

Mary slid a piece off the cookie sheet and onto a cooling rack. "Sure, sweetheart," she said. "But give it a minute to cool, okay?"

Timothy reached over and copied Bradley's actions, popping the still-hot treat into his mouth. "It's good," he said, waving into his mouth.

Margaret shook her head. "It's like having another child," she teased.

Mary felt the piece on the rack, and it had cooled down. "Okay, Clarissa, you can try it now," she said.

Clarissa bit into the flaky, cinnamon-sugar coated crust and closed her eyes in delight. "This is really good," she said. "Are we having this for Thanksgiving?"

"No," Mary said. "This is for tonight."

"Really?" Clarissa and Bradley both asked.

"Yes, really," she replied with a smile. "This is the reward for those who make the pies."

Bradley scooped up another piece. "Good thing I did the peeling," he said. "I qualify."

Clarissa started to speak when a noise caught her attention. She turned to see her kitten trying to climb into the fireplace. "Look," she laughed. "Lucky's attacking the chimney."

Mary turned to see the kitten standing on her hind legs pawing at the chimney. "That's odd," she said. "I wonder if something flew in."

She wiped her hands on a towel and then walked toward the fireplace. She was about to kneel down next to the kitten when a fat, ghost rat fell onto the cold, empty grate. "What in the world?" she exclaimed.

She jumped back, and a moment later a rush of white rats started to stream into the living room from the chimney. "Gross," she called out as Lucky tried to attack the phantom rodents.

"What? What's wrong?" Bradley asked rushing to her side. She grabbed his arm and he could see the deluge of the animals.

Suddenly, the ghost rats started coming up through the cold air register on the floor. Without thinking, Bradley grabbed a cushion from the chair and slammed it over the register, but the rats drifted through the cushion and continued spilling into the room.

"Mary, what's going on?" her mother cried.

"Mom, I...we..." she turned to look at Bradley and raised her hands in confusion.

"Ma, we've got a ghostly rodent issue," Bradley called out.

Reacting swiftly, Margaret covered all of the exposed food in the kitchen. "Mary, they must be wanting something from you," she called.

"Look, Lucky wants to go down into the basement," Clarissa said, turning toward the basement door.

"Clarissa, no," Mary called, but it was too late. The door was open, and another stream of rats were pouring into the house.

Mary stood up. "Ma's right," she said. "They want something from me."

"Mary, these are rats, not Lassie," Bradley said.

"I've read that lab rats are highly intelligent," Timothy inserted. "And the street rats in Chicago are nearly human."

"Ma, I'm going to go out with Bradley," Mary said. "I think they'll follow us."

"You go, darling," Margaret replied. "We'll put Clarissa to bed."

"But how will we know if all the rats are gone?" Clarissa asked, watching her kitten race around the room.

"Lucky will show us," Timothy said.

Mary and Bradley grabbed their coats, and Bradley pulled his gun out of the safe.

"Do you really think we're going to need that?" Mary asked.

Bradley shrugged. "Well, if it has anything to do with Granum, we just might."

They hurried from the house and were relieved to see that the rats were following them, pooling around the cruiser. "This is just plain gross," Bradley said as he helped Mary in the car.

"Could be worse," she said when he climbed in.

"How?" he asked when Mary placed her hand on his arm so he could continue to see them.

"They could have been experimenting on snakes or spiders."

Chapter Forty-two

Bradley put the cruiser in drive and slowly started down the street, trying to avoid hitting the rats.

"Bradley, they're dead," Mary reminded him. "It's okay to speed up."

He glanced at her and then shook his head. "Never a dull moment," he muttered, looking back at the road and accelerating.

She bit back a laugh and turned to watch the rats as they slowly moved from around the sides of the vehicle to in front of them. "I can't believe it," Mary said. "But it really does look like they're leading us."

"Pa, Timmy's in the well," Bradley said in a high-pitched squeaky, rodent-like voice.

Mary nearly choked as her laughter bubbled up. "Okay, you've had way too much sugar today," she said. Then she shook her head to clear it. "I've had too much sugar today too."

She looked far ahead to the front of the rat stampede and realized they were heading out of town. "I think they're leading us out of town," she said. "I bet you they're taking us to Granum."

"Well, that's not going to do us a whole lot of good," Bradley said. "Because Granum is locked up nice and tight for the holiday, and I don't think I can get a warrant issued because dead rats showed up at my house."

Mary nodded. "Yes," she sighed. "They'd probably lock you up."

She thought about it for a moment and then smiled. "Can you get hold of Alex?" she asked.

He nodded. "Yeah, give me a second," he said. He accessed his phone, and soon Alex' phone number was dialed and ringing.

"Boettcher," Alex answered.

"Hey, it's Bradley and Mary," Bradley said.

"What's up?"

Bradley glanced over at Mary and lifted his eyebrows. "You get to explain."

"Hi, Alex. We got a lead, and we need to get into Granum. Tonight. Actually, like in ten minutes," she said.

"Is it something I can get a warrant for?" he asked.

"Not unless the judge is Walt Disney," Bradley muttered.

"What?" Alex asked.

"Nothing," Mary said, shaking her head at Bradley. "But, no, it's nothing that will stand up in court. But I have another way."

"Okay. What?" Alex asked.

"Call Angela Tate and ask her to meet us and let us in," she said.

"Mary, tomorrow is Thanksgiving, not Christmas," Alex said. "You don't get presents like that."

"When you call her, just mention that you'd like her to open up Granum for us, or you'd like her to tell you about the medical approval procedure for having deviated septum surgery," Mary replied. "I'm sure she'd rather come down tonight."

"Is this some kind of code?" Alex asked.

"Something like that," Mary said. "And I think it'll work."

"Okay, I'll try it, and I'll call you back."

The phone disconnected, and Bradley pulled on to Highway 20, still following the rats. "Deviated septum surgery?" he asked her.

She shrugged. "Just girl talk in a bathroom," she replied.

"You learn a lot of stuff in bathrooms," he said, shaking his head in wonderment.

"I know, right?" she said with a knowing smile. "And that's why we always go in pairs, so we have a witness."

He grinned. "Well, I knew there had to be a logical reason."

The phone rang, and Bradley pressed the button to link it to the hands free device. "Alden," he said.

"I don't know what a nose job has to do with getting us entry to Granum," Alex said, "but she's going to meet us there in ten minutes. No questions asked." He paused. "Are you going to tell me more about this?"

"Not if I don't have to," she replied. "I think silence is a good trade for access."

"Okay, I'm leaving the house now," Alex said.

"We're almost there," Bradley replied. "But we will wait in the parking lot until you get there."

"Thanks," Alex replied. "And Mary, I'm glad you're on my side."

Mary smiled. "Thanks, Alex."

Chapter Forty-three

The rats were swarming the building when Mary and Bradley pulled up into the parking lot. One side of the building was covered with white ghost rats as they climbed up to the third floor and then disappeared into the windows.

"Third floor," Bradley said.

"There's no place like home," Mary replied. She looked around the parking lot. "But there aren't any cars here," she said. "I don't understand why they brought us here."

"Maybe they drew a map on one of the white boards, and they need to show it to us," Bradley suggested.

Mary's lips thinned as she looked at him. "You are not taking these rats seriously," she said.

"Did you just hear yourself?" he asked. "These are animals. Dead animals. I don't think they know what they're doing."

"They came all the way to our house to get us," Mary said. "They must have some kind of plan in mind."

Bradley was quiet for a moment and then finally turned to her. "Have you ever seen a horror flick where the people are consumed by trained rats?" he asked, his voice soft and ominous. Then he starting humming a song about a rat, made famous by Michael Jackson. "Ben…"

"Stop it," Mary insisted, rubbing her arms. "You are really creeping me out."

"Mary," he whispered. "I don't think we should go in there. Bad things could happen."

She lightly slapped his arm. "Okay, get serious," she said. "There really could be something to this."

He nodded. "And if there's not?" he asked.

She took a deep breath. "Do you have another pen you could lose?"

He chuckled and nodded. "Yeah, I do," he said.

Two cars pulled into the driveway, one right after the other. "Well, here's to the rats," Bradley said, and then he lowered his voice. "I hope they're not hungry."

"Stop it, Bradley Alden," Mary warned

They got out of their car and met Alex and Angela at the front door.

"This had better be good," Angela said.

"Oh, it's good alright," Bradley said, his tone serious and professional. "And we appreciate your cooperation."

She opened the front door and let them into the lobby. Walking over to the reception desk, she leaned over to the inside and flipped on a switch. The lobby was illuminated with lights. "So, where do you want to go?" she asked.

"The lab," Mary said. "We need to go upstairs to the lab."

They took the elevator up, and when the door opened, Mary saw a group of rats congregating in front of the elevator. They met her eyes and then turned and ran down the hall towards the lab, their squeaks echoing in the hall.

"What's that noise?" Angela asked.

"I didn't hear anything," Alex said.

Angela shook her head and then shrugged her shoulders. "Must be my imagination," she said.

Mary remembered when the rat had fallen on Angela in the lab and she had reacted to it. She wondered if Angela was sensitive to ghosts.

"No, I heard it, too," Mary said. "It sounded like squeaking."

Angela nodded. "Yes," she said, looking around. "That's right. I hope none of the rats have escaped."

Angela hurried down the hall towards the lab, Alex at her side and Mary and Bradley farther behind.

"I hadn't thought of that," Bradley whispered.

"What?" Mary asked, hoping she wouldn't be sorry for replying.

"What if it's a trap, and the dead rats have freed the live rats?" he said. "And they are all waiting to ambush us in the laboratory?"

She stopped walking and stared at him for a moment. "You do realize that your son can hear you, right?" she asked. "Do you really want Mikey to know his daddy torments his mommy?"

Bradley placed his hands on Mary's belly. "Shhhh, Mikey, don't listen," he whispered. Then he leaned forward and placed a quick kiss on Mary's lips. "Okay, no more tormenting. Let's go see what your rat friends want."

Chapter Forty-four

When Mary and Bradley turned the corner in the lab towards the work stations, Angela was already coming out of the rat room. "The rats are all caged up and quiet," she said. "I don't know what I could have been hearing."

But Mary knew. The workstations were covered with rats, climbing over each other and dropping off the ends of the desk as they swarmed the area.

"We need to go through the workstations," she said. "And I think we should start with Chandler's."

"Angela," Alex said. "Can you get us the password to his computer?"

She stared at him for a moment, and Mary saw him mouth the words deviated septum. Angela nodded quickly and left the room.

Alex turned to Mary. "That's a magic phrase," he said. "Do you think it will work on other women?"

Mary smiled. "No, I don't think so."

Bradley opened the drawers to the desk and found a number of hypodermic needles with a clear liquid inside of them. "What the hell is this?" he asked.

"Don't touch that," Angela called out. "It's ketamine."

"Isn't that a date rape drug?" Mary asked.

Alex nodded. "Well, it used to be," he said. "But it could still be found in the girl's system up to three days later. So now a newer, less traceable drug is being used."

"Yay for progress," Mary replied.

"Why would Chandler have ketamine in his workstation?" Bradley asked Angela.

"It's veterinary grade," she explained. "It can be used when we do experiments on the rats so they're more cooperative."

"But why isn't it in the rat room, instead of the drawer of his workstation?" Mary asked.

"Chandler," she paused. "Chandler has a unique way of working with the rats and, quite frankly, to prevent any problems from places like PETA, we just let him quietly have his way."

"That sounds very odd," Mary said.

Angela shrugged. "Well, they're just rats," Angela exclaimed. Several of the ghost rats standing close by squealed, and Angela quickly looked around. "Did you hear that?"

She hurried across the lab and entered the rat room again.

"I think we should pick Chandler up for questioning," Alex said.

"But we really don't have anything to go on," Mary said. "Other than his weird obsession with rats."

"And the fact he has date rape drugs in his desk," Alex said.

"Ruth wasn't raped or drugged," she said. "She was shot."

"But Chandler was the one who told her about the field next to Gund Cemetery," Bradley added.

"What?" Alex asked.

"Chandler was the one who suggested Ruth get samples from the field near the cemetery," Mary confirmed. "And this morning, I think I saw him leaving the cemetery."

Bradley nodded. "And my deputies dug up the bodies of dozens of rats."

"Okay, that's creepy," Alex said. "I think we need to, at the very least, talk to him."

Mary nodded. "Yeah, he's been on the top of my suspect list," she agreed. "I guess talking to him can't hurt."

"I'll have one of my guys pick him up and bring him into the station for questioning," Bradley said, and then he turned to Mary. "Do you want to come to the station or do you need me to drop you off at home?"

She looked at her watch. It was already past nine o'clock. "Actually, I'd really like to be there when you question him," she said.

"Okay," Bradley said. "Ready to go?"

She shook her head. "Sorry, just let me run to the bathroom first."

The third floor bathroom was now becoming familiar to Mary. She slipped inside the door and started to walk to a stall when Ruth appeared next to the counter.

"What are you doing here so late?" Ruth asked.

"Give me one minute," Mary said. "Then I can talk."

True to her word, a minute later Mary was at the counter, washing her hands. "We followed some clues that led us back here," Mary said.

"Were they good clues?" Ruth asked excitedly.

Mary nodded. "Well, I think we're getting closer," she said. "We're going to be picking up Chandler for questioning."

"Chandler?" Ruth asked, looking confused. "It can't be Chandler."

Chapter Forty-five

Chandler slipped the backpack off his shoulder and placed it on his kitchen counter. He hurried back to his door to make sure the deadbolt was in place. "Can't let anyone see what what's going on," he whispered to himself, "can I?"

Walking back to the kitchen counter, he pulled out the gallon-sized, plastic bags that contained the remains of the rats that had been used for experiments that day and placed them side by side on the counter.

"I'll take care of you guys tomorrow," he said. Then he looked down and noticed that one of the bags hadn't been sealed, and the rat inside was still twitching. "You really shouldn't be alive."

Sighing, he looked around the kitchen. "What am I going to do with you?" he asked, holding up the plastic bag and shaking his head. He put the rat down on the counter, unzipped another section of his backpack and pulled out a small vial with clear liquid. Then he pulled out a small syringe. "This will take care of you."

Sticking the needle into the top of the vial, he filled the syringe with a small amount of fluid. He turned back to the rat, still moving slightly in the plastic bag. "In one more minute," he said, sticking the needle through the plastic and into the body of the rat. "You will be asleep forever."

He emptied the drug into the rat's body, watching as its movements stilled and the rat stopped breathing. He smiled and nodded. "Okay then," he said.

He opened his refrigerator, which had an upper shelf with milk, some cheese and a couple cartons of yogurt, and slipped the plastic encased rats into the empty middle shelf. "It's just like a morgue," he said, as he placed them on the metal rungs. "You'll stay nice and fresh."

Once they were all inside, he closed the door and opened the freezer. He reached in and pulled out another container, a frozen pizza, and put it on the kitchen counter.

"Yes, pepperoni," he said to himself.

Walking across the kitchen, he turned on the small oven to preheat it and then went over to the sink to wash his hands. He pulled a knife out of the silverware drawer to slit the plastic covering the pizza and walked back over to the counter. He'd just inserted the tip of the blade into the plastic when the doorbell rang.

He glanced up at the clock and shook his head. It was about 8:30. Who could be dropping by?

Opening the door, he was more than a little surprised to see Charlie standing in the hallway. "Hey, Charlie," he said. "What's up?"

"I'm sorry to bother you," Charlie said. "But I'm pretty upset about Ruth's death, and I was just wondering, you know, if we could just talk for a little while."

Chandler smiled sympathetically and nodded. "Yeah, dude, sure," he said, opening the door to his apartment. "Come on in. I was just going to make a pepperoni pizza, you want some?"

Charlie nodded. "Yeah, that would be nice," he said. "Thank you."

"Hey, no problem," Chandler replied as he walked back to the counter. He looked over at the oven that was still preheating and turned back to Charlie. "You want something to drink? I got cola and root beer, nothing harder."

"A cola would be great," Charlie said after slipping off his coat and joining Chandler in the kitchen. "You know, as long as you're having something, too."

"Oh, sure," Chandler said, barely opening the refrigerator door to grab two cans of cola. "I'm ready for a caffeine boost. It's been a crazy day."

He put both cans on the counter, slid one over to Charlie and popped the opening on his own. But

232

before he could drink, Charlie put his hand out and stopped him. "You know, I was thinking that maybe we could do something special," he said.

Chandler put his soda on the counter. "Like what?"

"You know, like make a toast to Ruth and then chug our drinks," he said. "I think Ruth would like that. She used to like our chugging contests."

Smiling, Chandler nodded. "Hey, that's a great idea," he said. "Let's…"

The alarm went off on the oven to signal it was preheated.

"Oh, hey, go on and put the pizza in," Charlie said. "Then we can toast."

Nodding, Chandler cut the rest of the plastic covering, slipped the pizza and cardboard backing off the counter and walked over and placed the pizza in the oven. He set the timer for twelve minutes and went back to join Charlie.

"I didn't know you could cook, man," Charlie said.

Chandler grinned and shrugged. "Well, yeah, my mom kind of taught me," he said.

Charlie laughed and nodded. Then he held up his can. "To Ruth," he said. "Gone from our lives way too soon."

Chandler wiped a tear from his eye and sniffed loudly. Then he held up his can and touched it to Charlie's. "To Ruth," he said. "One of the nicest people I've ever known."

They clinked their cans one more time and then chugged down the contents without taking a break. Chandler slammed his can down on the counter and crushed it. "To Ruth!" he yelled.

Charlie followed suit. "To Ruth," he said, smashing his can, too, but only crumpling it slightly.

Chandler picked up the can and lobbed it across the room into the trash can. Charlie followed suit, bouncing his against the wall and then into the can.

"Score," Chandler cried, smiling at Charlie. Then Chandler grabbed the counter with both hands.

"What's wrong?" Charlie asked calmly.

"I don't feel good," Chandler stammered. "I don't feel good at all."

Charlie walked over to Chandler, put his arm around his waist and helped him to a chair. "Okay, just let me clean things up, and we can go for a ride," Charlie said.

"A ride?" Chandler groaned confused.

"Uh, huh," Charlie said as he walked over to the oven, pulled the pizza out and threw it in the garbage can. He walked back and then turned off the oven.

"Where do you keep your paper and pens?" Charlie asked.

"In my backpack," Chandler groaned and then clutched his stomach. "Dude, I feel really sick."

"Don't you know that you're never supposed to leave an open drink alone?" Charlie said casually as he pulled out a pen and paper and began to write. "Someone might put something into it."

"Charlie what are you doing?" Chandler asked, his eyesight becoming blurred.

"Oh. Well, we're going to go to the cemetery," Charlie said looking up from the paper.

"Not tonight," Chandler replied, his speech becoming more slurred. "I don't have to go until the morning."

Charlie shook his head, propped the note up on the edge of Chandler's backpack and shook his head. "No, Chandler," he said. "By tomorrow morning you will be dead. Just like Ruth."

Charlie walked over and pulled an incoherent Chandler to his feet. "Here we go," he said. "All you have to do is place one foot in front of the other."

"Charlie, I don't..." Chandler couldn't form any more words.

"See, Chandler, this is just how your rats feel," Charlie said. "Isn't it fitting that you're going to die in the same field as your rats?"

Chapter Forty-six

"Why can't it be Chandler?" Mary asked Ruth as they stood next to the counter in the bathroom.

"Because Chandler couldn't hurt a fly," Ruth said. "Much less point a gun at someone and shoot."

Mary shook her head. "Wait, didn't both you and Sonja joke about how Chandler was obsessed with killing the rats?" she asked.

Ruth closed her eyes for a moment and sighed. She opened her eyes and looked at Mary. "No, he didn't hurt them," she said. "He was obsessed about them being hurt. He hated when we had to use them for experiments, and he refused to let them be treated like garbage. He said they were warm-blooded creatures and they deserved a decent burial just like anyone else."

"Which is why he was at the cemetery so often," Mary replied.

Ruth nodded. "It is the closest cemetery to Granum," she said. "And he never buried them in the cemetery itself, only on the other side of the fence."

"Why did he have the ketamine at his workstation?" Mary asked.

"Because sometimes we couldn't use any anesthesia when we were testing the rats because it would jeopardize the results, so they were often in pain," she said. "Some of the interns would just leave them in their cage, suffering until they died. Chandler would go in and give them a shot of ketamine, which would stop the pain. Chandler said they would just go to sleep and that was a better way to die. He really cared about those little creatures."

No wonder the ghost rats stayed around Chandler. He was the one that saved them from suffering, Mary thought. But then why did they come to her house? And why did they lead her here?

"Which of the interns were cruel to the rats?" Mary asked, a sneaking suspicion in the corner of her mind.

"Charlie seemed to really enjoy making them suffer," Ruth said with a shrug. "But Charlie was kind of mean to people, too. He just didn't seem to like anyone."

"But, he said he would bring food to you when you were working at the lab," Mary replied.

Ruth shook her head. "He never did that," she said. "And if he did, I would worry that it was poisoned or something."

"I need to get back to Bradley," Mary said. "Can you come back with me?"

238

"Sure," she said. "I'll come with you."

Mary hurried back to the lab and found Alex and Bradley having a discussion with Angela.

"I don't think Chandler is our guy," Mary said plainly.

"Why not?" Alex asked.

Mary turned to Angela. "Angela, can you tell us what Chandler did to the rats?" Mary asked.

Angela shrugged. "He gave them the ketamine to make sure they didn't suffer when we put them down," she said. "But we have no liability here. We didn't buy the ketamine. Chandler pays for it by himself."

"He bought anesthesia for the rats, so they won't suffer?" Bradley asked.

Mary nodded. "And then, because he felt that any warm-blooded animal deserved a proper burial and not just a toss in the garbage can, he buried them outside the property limits of Gund Cemetery because that's the closest one to Granum."

Alex shook his head. "Okay, so he's sounding less and less weird," he admitted.

"But perhaps Angela would like to share what Charlie did with the rats," Mary said.

Angela shook her head. "I'm not down here most of the time," she replied easily. "I have no idea what the interns do."

"Except for the time she walked in on him abusing the rat," Ruth said.

"Except for the time you walked in on Charlie abusing one of the rats," Mary repeated.

Angela turned and stared at Mary. "How did you…" she paused and nodded. "Yes, there was one time when I entered the rat room and saw Charlie behaving in an overtly cruel manner to one of the lab rats."

"She interviewed us, and we told her he did it all the time," Ruth added.

"What did the other interns say when you interviewed them about Charlie's actions?" Mary asked.

Angela just stared at Mary for a long moment, and then she finally answered. "They told me it was common for Charlie to act like that," she said.

"Why didn't you fire him?" Mary asked.

"Because he threatened that he would go to PETA and let them know about the abuses we allowed the rats to suffer," she said. "He had recorded his abuses on his phone, without his face or voice, but with enough identifying material to implicate Granum. We had no choice."

"You had no choice, but to allow him to torture animals because Granum might have received some bad publicity?" Mary asked.

"That's the way it is in the real world," Angela said. "You have to make choices."

Bradley's phone rang, and he picked it up immediately. "What?" he asked. "Okay, stay put, and I'll call you right back." He looked up and met Mary's eyes. "Chandler isn't home. And my deputies said they found a suicide note."

"A suicide note?" Mary repeated. "That doesn't make sense. Why would Chandler want to commit suicide?"

Chapter Forty-seven

Charlie drove straight to the field next to Gund Cemetery, looking for a place to park that wouldn't leave tire tracks. He glanced over at the Visitor's Center, still busy with holiday travelers, and shook his head. Too many people.

He pulled his car around and headed back towards Highway 20. He turned left on the highway and drove to the first left turn, then pulled across the westbound lane and into the driveway of the farmer whose land abutted the cemetery. The house was several yards away from the drive, so after turning off his headlights, Charlie slowly drove down the gravel drive behind the house and outbuildings towards the harvested field.

A light turned on in the back of the house, so Charlie quickly turned off his car and waited. He was parked behind an older silo, beyond a large concrete pad that ran between a cluster of older, faded farm buildings. The house was north of the outbuildings, but smaller buildings created sight barriers between the back porch and the silo.

Charlie watched as the back door opened and a man armed with a flashlight came out onto his back porch. He slowly scanned the outbuildings, paying particular attention to the chicken coop. The flashlight missed the old silo, and Charlie breathed a sigh of relief. Finally, the man closed the door and the porch light was turned off.

His heart beating, Charlie took several deep breaths, calming himself and waiting for a little while before daring to turn his car back on again. He waited until several semitrailers rumbled down Highway 20 in front of the house before he started his car again. Once the engine was running, he held his breath and watched the door. Nothing.

Putting the car into gear, he turned down a dirt-packed, tractor lane that ran down the edge of the field. At the edge of the field, he flipped on his headlights and slowly drove down the land, the car being tossed back and forth as it traversed the uneven ground. Finally, he could see the cemetery fence in the distance. He stopped his car and turned to Chandler, who was unconscious in the seat next to him.

"We are really close to where Ruth was standing when I shot her," he said to Chandler, and then he shook his head. "You know, if she just hadn't been so smart. If she had just been more careless with her data. If her passwords had just been easier. I really didn't want to kill Ruth. I just needed her paper." He sighed. "When you look at it that way, it was really Ruth's own fault that she died."

He stepped out of the car, walked around to the trunk and opened it. Withdrawing a rifle case, he slipped it over his shoulder and then walked to the passenger door and opened it. "So, this is what we're going to do," he explained, slapping Chandler's face to wake him up.

Chandler started and then groaned softly.

"Good," Charlie said. "I've got your attention. So, we are going to take a little walk into the field, okay?"

Chandler nodded, rubbing his sore face. "Okay," he slurred.

"Then you're going to sit down and cross your legs," Charlie said, "so I can prop the gun between your legs and your mouth. Then I'll put your hand on the trigger, and all you have to do is pull the trigger. Okay?"

"Charlie, I don't feel good," Chandler moaned.

Charlie grinned. "Don't worry big guy," he said. "Soon you won't be feeling anything at all."

Chapter Forty-eight

Mary turned to Angela. "We need to get access to Charlie's workstation," she said.

"What?" Angela scoffed. "Why? If Chandler kills himself, the case is solved."

"Not if someone is actually trying to murder Chandler, too," Mary said. "Stanley mentioned that Charlie was very eager to give him information that implicated Chandler. If Charlie is the real killer, maybe he thinks he can get away with it by making it look like Chandler killed himself."

Bradley hurried over to Charlie's workstation and started pulling things out of the drawers while Angela turned on the computer, put in her administrator's password to bypass Charlie's security and waited for it to boot up.

Bradley opened the large bottom drawer on the side of the desk and pulled out a forest green backpack.

"That's my backpack," Ruth cried.

"That's Ruth's backpack," Mary said.

Bradley spread the backpack out on the table, and everyone could see the dark stain of blood across the back.

Angela stared at the backpack, her hands shaking. "He actually did it?" she asked, her voice high-pitched and nearly hysterical. "He actually killed her?"

Mary moved in next to Angela and opened Charlie's word processing system. She looked at his current files and found what she'd been searching for. "Here it is," she said. "Ruth's paper with Charlie's name inserted instead of Ruth's."

"That's all he wanted?" Ruth asked. "He killed me because he wanted my paper?"

"Where do you think he's taken Chandler?" Bradley asked.

Mary looked at the rats scurrying around the desks. Could they be smart enough to help them? They had led them back to Granum.

"Bradley, I need you to create some kind of diversion so I can talk to the rats," Mary whispered.

"Talk to the…" he began.

"Please," she begged.

"Look," Bradley called, hurrying to the window. "Is that something?"

Everyone hurried to the window except Mary. She turned to the rats. They looked up at her with their unblinking, pink eyes and white twitching whiskers. "Find Chandler. He needs your help. Go find Chandler."

They stared at her for a moment longer and then they started to move, slipping past the group and out through the window.

"I think I know where Chandler is," Mary said, praying she was right. "But we have to leave now."

They hurried from the room and down to the banks of elevators. "What did you do?" Bradley asked.

She looked up at him. "I said, go find Chandler, girl, go find Chandler," she said. "And they did."

"Well, you hope they did," Bradley countered.

She nodded. "Yes. Yes, I really do."

The elevator opened, and they hurried inside.

Chapter Forty-nine

Bradley's cruiser took the lead, while Mary looked out the window, trying to keep track of the rats in the dark. "They're heading toward Highway 20," she said, watching them scatter towards the busy intersection. Mary gasped in horror as a double-long semi-trailer barreled towards the creatures, only to sigh in relief as it passed through their ghostly bodies without the slightest degree of harm.

"I keep forgetting they're dead," she said, her voice slightly shaking.

"Yeah, I know what you mean," Bradley replied. "They're like this undulating wave of rodents."

She grinned. "That's kind of beautiful and disgusting all at the same time."

He chuckled. "Okay, the road's clear. Which way now?"

"They're cutting across the field," Mary said, watching them. "It looks like they're going towards Gund Cemetery."

"Well, we're not cutting across country," Bradley said, turning left onto the west-bound lane on Highway 20. "We'll cut them off at the pass."

Mary looked over her shoulder. "Alex is right behind us," she said.

"Good. It would be nice if we both make it to the cemetery at the same time," Bradley said.

They turned right on the road that led to the cemetery. "You might want to pull into the gravel road that goes all the way to the back of the cemetery," Mary said. "That will get us closer to the end of the field, and that's where Chandler was burying the rats."

Bradley called Alex. "We're going to pull into the cemetery road," Bradley said when Alex answered. "And drive to the end of the road for better access."

"I think I saw someone on the edge of the field," Alex said. "So, be alert."

They pulled into the cemetery and sped down the gravel lane.

"I see someone," Mary said, peering out the window. "At the far end of the field."

Bradley pulled the cruiser up next to the fence and jumped out of the car. "Stay here," he said to Mary. "Whoever killed Ruth used a rifle, and I don't want you out there."

She started to argue, then stopped. He needed to get out there, and he didn't need to worry about her. "Go," she said. "I'll stay here."

"Thank you," he said, pulling his handgun from his belt. "I'll be back as soon as I can."

He started to close the door when she stopped him. "Bradley," she called.

He turned back to her, his face questioning.

"There's a break in the fence at the northeast corner of the cemetery," she said. "It's the quickest way into the field."

He smiled at her. "Thanks."

Mary watched him slip through the fence opening and head toward the lone figure walking along the tree line. Suddenly, a movement to the side of the cruiser caught her eye. The rats were swarming around a furrow in the field, in the same area Mary had found Ruth's body. She looked over to the edge of the field where Bradley and Alex were following the suspect. There was nothing she could do to get their attention without alerting the person they were following.

Shaking her head, Mary reached up to make sure the interior lights were turned off. Then she quietly opened the car door and slipped outside. Following Bradley's path, she slipped through the opening in the fence line and then turned back toward the road. The ground was bumpy, and Mary had to carefully feel her way forward. As she got closer to the swarm, she was able to see a body on the ground.

"Oh, no," she exclaimed softly. "Chandler."

Hurrying forward, she pushed through the swarm to get to the young man. As she got closer, she could hear his quiet sobs.

"Chandler?" she asked.

"I don't want to die," he cried.

"Well, of course you don't," she said as she got closer.

"Don't!" he cried out. "Don't move any closer."

She froze and looked around. A thick rope encircled the area, looped around jagged cornstalks, ending finally with Chandler.

"Where does the rope end?" she asked.

"It's rigged to the rifle's trigger," he whimpered. "The hammer is cocked, and the muzzle is pointed at my head."

"Can you move?" she asked.

"No, the rope is also wrapped around my body," he said. "If I move, it shoots me. And I've got to say, the drugs Charlie gave me are making me pretty drowsy."

"Well, crap," Mary said, slowly walking around the circumference of the rope trap, making sure she was far enough away that she couldn't upset anything. "You need to stay awake!" She stared at him from a different direction. "There has to be a way to move the gun."

"Only if you can lift the gun in the air without putting any pressure on the ropes from any other direction," Chandler said.

"How about putting something in between the hammer and the firing pin?" Mary asked, moving so she was behind the butt of the gun and looking at Chandler's face.

"That could work," Chandler said. "But if the rope gets touched, it's all over."

The rope was intertwined all over, and Mary knew there was no way she could disarm the gun in the dark. She looked around, trying to find something that would work. She backed away from Chandler, slipping through the swarm of rats.

"How smart are lab rats?" she asked Chandler, trying to keep him talking and alert.

"I think they're just as smart as dogs," he replied. "I even taught some of them tricks."

She stopped and looked at him. "You taught them tricks?"

"Yeah, they learn even faster than a dog," he said. "I actually taught them fetch."

Mary, who was still looking around searching for an idea to save him, stopped when she noticed several of the rats chewing on scattered kernels of corn on the ground. "Which rats did you train?" she asked.

Chandler sighed. "Lucy, Linus and Snoopy," he said. "But they were killed last week. They're buried by the cemetery."

"Lucy. Linus. Snoopy," Mary called, and three of the rats looked towards her.

Kneeling down she picked up a few of the corn kernels. "Fetch," she called, tossing the corn a few feet.

The ghost rats darted across the uneven ground and sniffed around until they found the kernels.

"What are you doing?" Chandler asked.

"I'm hoping these rats are as smart as you think," she said.

Chapter Fifty

Bradley moved forward into the tree line that separated the field from the edge of the property line. He could see a dark clothed figure in front of him, moving slowly. Had he not heard their cars pull up? Was he so sure of his plan that he wasn't even worried about it? Bradley jogged forward, getting closer to the suspect. The guy wasn't even looking over his shoulder. Why was he so confident?

A hand on his shoulder had Bradley bracing for a fight. "It's me," Alex whispered, jogging forward to walk next to him. "What's with this guy?"

"I don't know," Bradley said. "He's not even looking over his shoulder."

Alex shrugged. "Let's take him," he said.

"Are you sure?" Bradley asked. "You could get your suit dirty."

Alex grinned. "Yeah, I never liked this suit anyway."

The two men rushed forward, Bradley tackling low and Alex hitting high. The suspect tumbled onto the ground rolling away from them. Bradley jumped after him, rolling him over and pinning him down. Charlie lashed out, kicking and punching, but Bradley held him tight.

"You have the right…" Bradley started and then stopped. Alex heard an audible sigh.

"Really?" Bradley exclaimed, holding up a set of earphones and a phone. "He was wearing ear phones."

Alex shook his head and walked over to Bradley. "I'll take those," he said. "You read him his rights."

Bradley handed Alex the electronics and then pulled Charlie to his feet. "You have the right to remain silent," Bradley said as he pulled his handcuffs out of their holder and clapped them over Charlie's wrist. "Anything you say can and will be used against you in a court of law. You have the right to an attorney. If you cannot afford an attorney, one will be provided for you. Do you understand the rights I have just repeated to you?"

He shook Charlie's arms. "Do you understand the rights I have just repeated to you?"

"Yeah. I'm not stupid," Charlie spat. "I get it."

"And with these rights in mind, do you wish to speak to me?" Bradley asked him.

"You've got nothing on me. I'm not afraid to talk to you," Charlie said dismissively. "I've done nothing wrong. Chandler asked me to tie him up. I didn't do anything."

255

"We're not talking about Chandler," Alex said. "We're talking about Ruth."

Charlie shook his head. "Like I told the old guy," he said. "Chandler did it. Chandler killed Ruth, and that's why he wanted to die."

"We found Ruth's backpack in your workstation drawer," Alex said. "And we found her research on your computer with your name on it. We've got you."

"Well, you're too late. Chandler already took the fall for her death," he said. "I know how this works. You got a fall guy. You don't need anyone else."

"Obviously you don't know how this works," Bradley said. "Because we don't want a fall guy, we want the murderer."

"So tell us where Chandler is," Alex demanded.

Charlie laughed, the sound sending chills down both of their backs. "He's all tied up," he said, laughing again. "And don't try to help him. The gun's rigged to not only discharge, but also give a little extra something special for anyone trying to help him."

Bradley grabbed Charlie's collar. "Where is he?" he said through gritted teeth. "Where's Chandler?"

Charlie motioned with his head. "Right where Ruth fell," he said with a shrug. "I thought it would be poetic justice."

Suddenly the sound of a rifle shot and a secondary explosion echoed in the night sky.

Charlie chuckled. "Guess he got help."

"Mary," Bradley breathed.

When he shoved Charlie into Alex's hands, Alex could see that Bradley's face was white with fear. "Go," Alex said, urging Bradley on. "I've got this."

Chapter Fifty-one

Bradley sprinted down the gravel lane and then dove through the tree line towards the field. Branches scraped against his face, but he wasn't even aware of the pain they were inflicting. All he could think of was Mary. In his mind, all he could picture was Mary lying on the cold ground in the middle of the field, her life ebbing away from her.

"Don't be hurt," he pleaded. "Oh, God, don't let Mary be hurt."

He emerged from the tree line gasping for air, but he continued on, his flashlight scanning the field. He ran, nearly twisting his ankles, over rough and uneven ground towards the place where they'd found Ruth's body. Finally, the beam of his flashlight illuminated the tops of figures above a furrow. But from his vantage, they didn't seem to be moving.

He pushed himself, jumping the furrows and finally gasping out her name. "Mary," he cried. "Mary."

"We're over here."

The sound of her voice nearly brought him to his knees. He took a deep, gasping breath. "Are you okay?" he asked. "I heard...I heard a gunshot."

He stumbled over the last furrow, finally next to her. Dropping to his knees, he pulled her into his arms and just held on to her.

"I'm sorry…" she began.

"Shhhh," he pleaded. "Just let me hold you for a moment."

She relaxed against him, feeling the rapid beating of his heart against her ear and waited, waited until his heart beat had slowed, waited until his grasp wasn't as tight, and waited until the tears she felt falling on her face slowed. Finally, when she heard him take a deep breath, she pulled away.

"I'm fine," she said softly. "I guess when I tossed the gun away from us the corn must have gotten dislodged."

Bradley shook his head. "Corn?"

Before she could respond, a triumphant yell sounded next to them. "I'm free," Chandler yelled, waving his arms in the air with rope still hanging from his wrists. "They did it. They actually did it."

He turned to Mary and Bradley. "Who would have thought that dead rats were as smart as live ones?" he said, his eyes wide with excitement. "Can people, like, study working with dead animals? Is that a thing?"

Mary grinned up at Bradley and then turned to Chandler. "I have a friend who's a professor," she said. "I'll get you his information, and you can talk to him about it."

"Cool," he said, leaning forward to untie his legs. "That is so cool."

Bradley stood up and helped Mary to stand. Then he led her a few yards away from Chandler. "You were supposed to stay in the car," he whispered.

She nodded. "I know, and I would have, really," she said. "But I saw the rats swarming, and then I saw Chandler. You were too far away for me to call, so…"

He bent over and kissed her. "So, you really had no other choice," he said.

She shrugged. "Yeah, kind of," she answered. "Did you catch Charlie?"

"Yeah, we tackled him," Bradley said. "And he actually confessed to Ruth's murder. So, it's going to be a fairly easy case for Alex."

"Good," Mary said. "I'm glad it's over. I…"

She stopped when she saw Ruth standing next to Chandler in the field. "I told you he didn't do it," Ruth said to Mary.

"You were right," Mary whispered. "He really is a good guy."

Ruth sighed. "Yeah, he was a good friend," she said. She paused for a moment, pondering something, and finally spoke again. "I guess it's time for me to go."

Mary nodded. "Yes," she said. "It's time for you to move on."

"My parents are still really sad," she said.

"And they are probably going to be sad for a long time," Mary replied. "Losing someone you love is hard."

"Do you know, will I be able to visit them?" Ruth asked. "Just to make sure they're okay?"

Smiling, Mary nodded. "Yes, from what I've seen, Heavenly Father keeps those bonds of love and family strong, even after death," she explained. "And those bonds often pull our loved ones back to the earth to check on us."

"Are they going to be okay?" Ruth asked.

Mary sighed. "That's kind of up to them," she said. "But I think they'll be fine."

"So, what do I do next?" Ruth asked.

"Look around," Mary replied. "Do you see a bright light?"

Ruth nodded. "Yeah, over by the cemetery. It's cool. It's kind of glowy and warm."

"Just walk towards that light," Mary said. "And as you get closer, you'll remember what you're supposed to do."

"Thanks, Mary," she said. "Will you tell my parents that I really love them? And tell Sonja that she was the best roommate anyone could ever have. And tell Chandler..." she paused for a moment and wiped a tear from her cheek. "Tell Chandler that I was lucky to be his friend."

"I will," Mary replied.

Mary watched Ruth glide towards the cemetery and then slowly fade away.

"Ruth was here, wasn't she?" Chandler asked, walking up to Mary and gazing over at the cemetery.

"Yes, she was," Mary said. "And she asked me to tell you that she was lucky to have you as a friend."

He shook his head. "No, I was the lucky one."

Chapter Fifty-two

Bradley pulled the cruiser into the driveway and looked over at Mary, sound asleep in the passenger seat. He really hated to wake her, but she needed to sleep in a bed, not a car. He got out of the car and walked over to the passenger side and opened her door. "Sweetheart," he whispered. She smiled in her sleep and snuggled further into the upholstery. "Sweetheart, you need to wake up just enough for me to help you upstairs."

"Okay," she murmured, not moving from her position.

He shook his head. "I really hate to do this," he said, pulling out his phone. He accessed the same application he'd used at Granum to block any listening devices, but this time he accessed a noise that was water running. Once it loaded, he held it close to her.

The sounds of water dropping, dribbling and flowing surrounded her, and suddenly Mary's eyes shot open wide. She turned to Bradley, her voice urgent. "Thank goodness we're home," she said, her voice still a little drowsy. "I really have to go to the bathroom."

He helped her from the car and into the house. She hurried to the bathroom on the first floor while he turned off the application on his phone. "Works every time," he laughed softly.

A few minutes later she came out of the bathroom and yawned widely. "I'm so tired," she said. "But there's something I still have to do tonight."

Bradley shook his head. "No, there's nothing you have to do tonight," he said, "but sleep."

"I can't. I made a promise, and I can't break it," she said.

He put his arm around her and helped her up the stairs. "Mary, you will be exhausted tomorrow if you don't get some sleep," he said. "Whatever it is can wait until the morning."

"But…" she began.

He turned her towards him and kissed her softly. "I love you," he said.

"That's not fair," Mary whispered.

He smiled and kissed her again. "I know," he said, leading her to their bedroom. "But tonight you are going to sleep right beside me so I can hold you and try to forget the horror I felt when I thought I'd lost you."

She looked up at him. "Bradley," she began.

He stopped and kissed her again. "I love you, Mary O'Reilly Alden," he said. "And right now, we are going to bed."

Chapter Fifty-three

Mary woke the next morning to find the space next to her in bed was already empty. She glanced at the clock. It was already eight-thirty. How could they let her sleep so late? She hurried to the bathroom and then threw on her robe to hurry downstairs, her hair askew and sleep still in her eyes.

"Ma," she called as she came down the stairs. "How could you…"

She froze on the steps when she heard Bradley's voice. "Darling, before you come down, I just want to let you know that your brothers and Ian and Gillian are already here," he said.

He walked over to the staircase and started up the stairs to meet her. "In case you weren't quite put together," he added in a whisper.

She put her hand to her head, felt her hair and took a couple of steps backwards. "How bad…" she stared.

He followed her up and stood on a step below her so they were face to face. "You look like you just tumbled out of bed," he whispered roughly, "which is one of the sexiest things I've ever seen." He reached up and stroked her cheek. "And if we didn't have a house filled with friends and family, I would show you just how much I want you right now."

She smiled and leaned forward, placing a kiss on his cheek, then moving back. "I haven't brushed my teeth yet," she said, scrunching her nose. Then her smiled widened. "So, I look pretty bad?"

He grinned back. "You're a hot mess," he said.

She laughed aloud and nodded. "Okay, I'm going back up to shower," she said. "How's Thanksgiving? Are we going to have to eat delivery pizza?"

"Your mom called Rosie last night and told her what was going on," Bradley said. "Rosie came over at six, and she and your mother have been in the kitchen doing magical things all morning."

Relief flowed over Mary, and she felt tears fill her eyes. "How come I'm so lucky?" she asked.

He shrugged. "Because you're married to me," he teased. "Now go upstairs and get ready. You have a half-hour before the parade starts."

She leaned forward and kissed him again. "Okay, I'm going."

Twenty minutes later, a showered, dressed and polished Mary came down the stairs, feeling much more confident to face the day. As she stepped from the staircase, the doorbell rang. "I'll get it," she called, and she turned to open the door.

"Joyce? Bill?" Mary asked, stunned to see Jeannine's parents standing on her front porch.

"Who is it, Mary?" Bradley asked, coming up behind her. "Joyce and Bill! What a surprise."

Joyce reached out and took Mary's hand in hers. "I hope it's not too much of an imposition for us to come for Thanksgiving," she asked.

Mary's eyes filled with tears, and she shook her head. "No," she said, her voice filled with emotion. "It's not an imposition at all. It's a…it's a…" She wiped her hands over her face to get rid of the tears and try to get hold of her emotions. Finally, she just gave up and threw her arms around Joyce. "I'm so glad you're here."

Bradley ushered them inside. "There's someone I think you should meet first," he said. "Then you can meet everyone else."

Mary stood with them, holding both of their hands as they waited next to the front door for Bradley to return. A moment later Bradley came from the kitchen holding Clarissa's hand.

"Hi," Clarissa said. "Are you coming for Thanksgiving?"

Joyce nodded as her eyes filled with tears and her lips quivered with emotion. "Yes," she whispered. "Yes we are."

"Great," Clarissa replied. "'Cause we've got lots of food."

"Do you, young lady?" Bill asked, his voice tight. "Well that's good to hear because I'm hungry."

"Clarissa," Mary said. "This is even better than you think. These are your grandparents. These are your mommy Jeannine's mommy and daddy."

Clarissa's eyes opened wide. "For real?" she asked.

"For real," Joyce replied, her voice shaky.

"So, I have more people who love me?" she asked.

Tears flowed unchecked down Joyce's cheeks as she nodded and bent down. "Yes, sweetheart, you do," she said. "You certainly do."

Clarissa launched herself into her grandmother's arms, and Bill bent over and held them both in his embrace. Mary laughed softly when she met Bradley's eyes and saw the tears in them, too. "Happy Thanksgiving," she whispered.

He smiled at her. "Yeah, it is."

Chapter Fifty-four

Arm in arm, Mary walked Joyce into the kitchen a few minutes later to introduce her to the rest of the family. Mary was surprised when Joyce slipped away from her and enfolded Margaret in a hug.

"Thank you," Joyce whispered to Margaret. "You were right."

Margaret hugged her again. "I'm so happy to see you here," she said, "where you and Bill belong."

Timothy came forward and shook Bill's hand. "It's grand to meet you," he said. "We're to watch the parade in a few moments and then take the kiddies to the park for a game of football. Would you be interested?"

Bill smiled. "Sounds like a lot of fun," he said.

"It is," Timothy said with a warm smile. "We grandpas get to sit on the sidelines and yell at the young men and tell them what's what."

Bill's smile widened. "Now, that sounds like even more fun."

Rosie came over to Mary and gave her a quick hug. "I hope you don't mind that I came over early," she said. "Your mother told me what an adventurous night you had. Goodness, I can't believe you're on your feet."

"I am so grateful that you came over," Mary said. "I really don't know what I'd do without you and Ma."

"Well, dear, that's what we're here for," Rosie said. "Now, we didn't want to take away all of the fun, so we left the Parker rolls and the corn pudding for you. The turkey's in the oven, the pies are all done and," she leaned closer and whispered, "Clarissa's cake is in the basement, staying cool."

The quilt, Mary thought with a sigh. *There's no way I'll be able to get it done on time.*

"Are you all right?" Rosie asked.

Mary nodded. "Yes, there was a project I was working on, and I just don't think I'm going to be able to finish it," she said, trying not to sound sad.

Rosie smiled. "Well, don't worry, dear," she said. "Things always work out the way they should."

Mary nodded mutely and then moved back into the fray of family, introducing Joyce to the rest of the group.

"You're looking radiant, darling," Ian said, placing a kiss on her cheek. "How's the wee bairn?"

"I think he's either a gymnast or a ninja," she said with a smile. "He's moving all the time."

"Ah, well, he's probably just practicing a good Scottish jig for when he's wearing the kilt I bought him," Ian teased.

Mary stared at him, her brows furrowing. "So, it's your fault he keeps me up all night," she teased back.

"Ach, no, you're right. It must be the ninja moves," Ian said, lifting his hands in surrender. "I'm certain no self-respecting Scot would be dancing the jig all night long."

"Iffen there was such a thing as self-respecting and Scot in the same sentence," Stanley said to Ian with a chuckle.

"Well, certainly not the one who'd be seen with you," Ian replied easily.

"You've been seen with me a time or two," Stanley countered.

Ian grinned. "And who would be calling me self-respecting?" he asked with a laugh.

Stanley chuckled. "Well, I'll keep being seen with you," he said, "as long as we don't have to have any disgusting, Scot-like food for dinner."

Ian turned and winked at Mary. "And did you get the makings for the Thanksgiving haggis?" he asked.

Mary nodded. "Oh, yes, and Rosie agreed that it would be much better to serve haggis instead of turkey and stuffing," she replied. "It's in the oven now."

Stanley studied Ian and then Mary and shook his head. "If there ain't an animal what said, gobble, gobble, gobble afore he died in that oven, there's gonna be trouble."

"Do sheep say gobble, gobble, gobble?" Mary asked.

"Aye, in Scotland we train them to do that," Ian replied. "And they also fly on occasion."

"Well, this ain't Scotland," Stanley grumbled. "And there weren't any Scots at the first Thanksgiving."

Ian looked surprised. "You don't know?" he asked.

Stanley eyed Ian suspiciously. "What?"

"About Myles Standish," Ian said.

Stanley placed his hands on his hips. "What about Myles Standish?"

Ian leaned forward and whispered. "He was Scottish, from the Isle of Mann, he was."

"That ain't so," Stanley said, shaking his head.

Ian shrugged. "Look it up," he replied.

"Fine, I will," Stanley grumbled. He looked around. "Bradley, do you have a computer I can use?"

"Sure, Stanley," Bradley replied. "You can use my tablet."

"Well, I guess we'll see what's what," Stanley said to Ian before he sauntered across the room.

"Was Myles Standish really Scottish?" Mary asked Ian quietly.

Ian shrugged. "No one's really sure," he said with a smile. "But he did own property that he inherited on the Isle of Mann, so he could have been Scottish."

"You are so bad," Mary said.

Ian chuckled. "Aye, and Stanley loves it."

Mary nodded. "Yes, he does," she agreed.

Chapter Fifty-five

A few minutes later, the front door opened and Katie Brennan walked in. "Okay, cinnamon rolls and parade at my house," she called.

Mary shook her head. "What?"

Katie shrugged. "Oh, we have a little surprise for you," she said. "Bradley and I decided that the men and the kids should watch the parade at my house, and then go straight to football from there."

"Okay, everyone," Bradley called, "grab your coats and off we go."

"Clifford is waiting on the front porch for you," Katie said to Bradley, slipping off her coat. "Have fun."

Bradley hurried over and gave Mary a quick kiss. "What?" she asked, still confused.

"Katie will fill you in," he said. "Love you."

The room was emptied in less than a minute. Mary stood, a little dazed, in the middle of the kitchen. "What just happened?"

"Are they gone?" Margaret O'Reilly called from upstairs.

When did Ma go upstairs? Mary wondered.

"Yes," Katie called. "You can bring it down."

Mary watched in wonder as Margaret and Rosie carried the quilting frame downstairs and set it up in the middle of the room. Margaret smiled at her daughter. "We thought we could all give you a hand with this," she explained.

Mary felt tears threaten again. "I don't think I've ever been this emotional about Thanksgiving before," she teased, wiping away a few stray tears. "Thank you so much."

They all pulled chairs around the frame, and Katie threaded needles, handing them out to the group.

"I'm so glad Katie is threading these needles," Rosie said, accepting hers from Katie. "My eyes aren't what they used to be."

Margaret laughed and nodded. "I was handing Mary needles and thread for me quite a few years ago," she confessed. "I think they're making the holes smaller these days."

Katie chuckled. "Well, we're going to have to teach Maggie and Clarissa how to quilt so we have needle threaders in our future," she said.

"Do you really think we could get them to sit still long enough to quilt?" Mary asked.

276

"I used to quilt when Jeannine was little," Joyce said, pushing her needle into the fabric. "She and I would sit and quilt together."

"That must be why she started this quilt for Clarissa," Mary said. "She was carrying on a legacy."

Joyce wiped a tear away. "Thank you for letting me do this with you," she whispered to Mary. "It means a great deal."

"It means a great deal to me that you came," Mary said. "We've all missed having you and Bill in our lives."

With the sounds of the Thanksgiving Parade in the background and the smells of dinner cooking in the oven, the women chatted and stitched the quilt until it was completely finished.

"Now all we have to do is sew on the edging," Joyce said with a smile. "What if we do it by hand, too?"

"Sure," Rosie said. "That shouldn't take any time at all. And I always think stitching done by hand lasts longer than a machine."

Katie nodded. "We could use a blind stitch," she suggested. "Or even a ladder stitch."

"Oh, a blind stitch would be lovely," Rosie said, "especially with this satin binding."

Mary looked over at her mother and smiled. "Perhaps while you are all blind and ladder stitching, I could start forming the Parker House rolls."

Rosie looked surprised. "Are you sure?" she asked. "This is the fun part."

Mary chuckled. "Oh, I am completely sure," she said. "But I am thrilled to know the quilt is in such capable hands."

She pushed her chair away from the table and walked into the kitchen. Her mother joined her a moment later.

"It's strange," Mary said, her voice lowered so it wouldn't reach the other room.

"What's strange?" Margaret asked.

"It's strange that you and Joyce seem like old friends and yet you only met her for a quick moment at the funeral."

Margaret caught the twinkle in her daughter's eye and smiled. "Isn't that the oddest thing?" she chuckled.

Mary hugged her mom. "Thank you for whatever you did," she said.

"I didn't do a thing," Margaret insisted. "I only issued an invitation."

Mary could hear the soft chatter and the laughter coming from the other room. She started to walk to the refrigerator when she felt the hairs on the back of her neck stand up. Turning, she went back towards the living room and gasped softly. Jeannine's ghost was standing next to the quilt and looked over at Mary, her eyes filled with joy and gratitude.

Suddenly Joyce stopped sewing and looked up. Tears filled her eyes. "I don't know what's wrong with me," she exclaimed, wiping away the moisture. "But for a moment I felt like my Jeannine was here with us."

Mary nodded. "Me, too," she whispered. "Me, too."

Chapter Fifty-six

The quilt was wrapped up and hidden, and the rest of the Thanksgiving preparations were complete. The furniture had been pushed back, and several large, folding tables were set up in the living room with an assortment of chairs from the various households. White tablecloths covered the tables, and an assortment of colored-paper leaves and turkeys were scattered in the middle of the tables for the centerpieces.

Bradley carried the turkey out into the living room and set it in the center of the table.

"Right after we take a picture, it's going back in the kitchen," Margaret said, "so we can carve it correctly."

Mary smiled and nodded. "Okay, everyone gather together so we can say a blessing."

Bradley looked around the room at those assembled, and then he turned to Bill. "Bill, I would be honored if you would say the blessing," he said.

"Are you sure?" Bill asked.

Bradley placed his hand on his former father-in-law's shoulder. "I'm more than sure," he replied.

Bill looked around the table at all the people gathered together before he bowed his head and began his prayer. "Dear God," he prayed. "As we come together to celebrate this day of Thanksgiving, we are grateful for the many blessings thou hast given us. We are grateful for family. We are grateful for new friends. We are grateful for love and kindness. We are grateful for forgiveness. We are grateful for all the hands that worked together to create this feast before us. We pray that thou wilt bless us this day. Bless our loved ones who are not with us. Bless those who mourn that they may be comforted. Bless those who serve us in the armed forces, that they and their families will be safe. And finally, God, bless this Thanksgiving dinner. Amen."

After an echoed chorus of "Amen," the noise level raised as dishes were passed and plates were filled. Rosie and Margaret brought platters of white and dark meat to the table. Mary placed several baskets of Parker House rolls strategically on the tables. Small card tables were set up to hold extra dishes that couldn't fit on the tables, and extra napkins were rushed from one end of the room to the other when a glass of milk was spilled.

"T'weren't my fault," Stanley grumbled as he sopped up the milk with a wad of paper napkins. "I was reaching for a roll, and the glass caught on my shirt."

Mary chuckled and shook her head. "My mother always said that it wasn't a true dinner until someone spilled their milk."

Then she turned and looked at Bradley's plate. "Um, you're missing something," she said.

He looked down at this overflowing plate and shook his head. "I can't fit another thing on it," he said.

"You haven't tried the corn pudding," she said. "And you did promise."

He sighed. "Fine," he replied, looking around. "Where is it?"

Mary looked and saw that it was on a side table near the other end of the table. "Why don't you just try a bite of mine," she offered.

"Really?" he asked with a smile. "That will work?"

"Yes," she said, biting back a smile. "That will work."

He brought his fork over to her plate and picked up a small bite of corn pudding and tasted it. His eyes widened, and he brought his fork back down onto her plate, bringing back a larger bite this time. "This is corn pudding?" he asked. "This stuff is great."

He looked up across the table. "Um, Sean, could you do me a favor and pass me the dish of corn pudding?"

"You want me to pass it to you like the pass you made this afternoon?" Sean asked with a smile. "Just about took my hands off."

"Sean O'Reilly," Margaret said. "We do not throw food."

"Don't worry, Ma," Art said. "Even if he wanted to throw it, he couldn't make it past his own salad plate."

"Says the guy who missed every single pass," Sean countered.

"Says the guy who throws like a girl," Tom inserted.

"Excuse me?" Mary asked.

"Present company excluded of course," Tom quickly replied, reaching over and passing the corn pudding towards Bradley.

"You're not just doing this to make me happy, are you?" Mary asked, turning to her husband.

He leaned over and kissed her quickly. "No, I'm not," he said. "You were right. This really is great."

The dish made its way to Bradley, and he scooped out a portion on his plate and replaced the amount he took on Mary's plate. "We have to make this more often."

Mary nodded. "Yes. Yes, we do."

Chapter Fifty-seven

The food had been put away, the dishes had been done, and Bradley had taken the kids out to the backyard to play games.

"Peek out the window and make sure they're all occupied," Rosie said as she carried the cake from the basement door towards the table.

"Aye, they have Bradley and Clifford tied up," Ian said, peeking through the blinds. "It looks like they might be building a wee fire underneath their feet."

"Aren't kids amazing?" Sean teased, standing alongside him. "Look! They're using a blow torch to get the flames going."

"But don't worry. Art and Tom are helping them, so the knots are good and tight," Ian said.

Sean looked from the window to Mary. "I didn't know you had a container of gasoline back there," he said. "That's going to hurt."

Mary shrugged calmly. "Well, it's a good thing that both Clifford and Bradley stated in their wills that if anything were to happen to them, both you and Ian would have to step in to be the father-figures," she said. "I'm sure you two could handle…" She paused. "How many kids?"

Ian stood up. "Well, now, if that's the case, I think I'll be going out there and looking out for my future," he laughed.

"Yeah, me, too," Sean added.

They walked over to the kitchen counter. Ian picked up two cans of aerosol whipping cream and handed one to Sean. "You don't go out to tame the beasties without some kind of weapon," he said.

Sean looked down at the can in his hand. "This is a weapon?" he asked.

Ian grinned. "Well, there's fighting, and then there's conquering," he replied.

"Yeah, and you Scots were always so good at conquering," Sean teased.

Ian stopped at the door and looked at Sean. "And have you not seen Braveheart?" he asked.

He opened the door wide, the whipping cream in his outstretched hand, and yelled, "FREEDOM!" Then he dashed down the stairs into the yard.

Sean walked more casually toward the door and shook his head. "Should I remind him that the Scots lost?"

He stepped outside and pulled the door behind him. But his voice could still be heard in the kitchen when he yelled, "Go Bears!"

The women stood in place until he closed the door. Then they all ran to the window.

"Oh, that's gross," Margaret said with a chuckle as they watched Ian and Sean squirt whipped cream into the eager, open mouths of the children.

"Ian's going to be a great dad," Mary said softly to Gillian.

"Aye, he is," she replied, shaking her head. "And our children will be spoiled brats."

A thump on the basement door brought them all to attention. "What the…" Margaret asked, hurrying to the door and opening it.

Timothy stood on the other side, the wooden dollhouse in his hands. "I thought we might want to set this up on one of the wee tables," he said.

"I'll help you," Bill volunteered.

Fifteen minutes later, the presents were in place, the candles were lit and everyone but Bradley and Clarissa were inside, waiting for the special event.

Taking a deep breath, Mary walked to the back door, opened it and called out. "Bradley, Clarissa, you both need to come inside right away."

Everyone hid, and Mary flicked off the lights.

"What's wrong?" Clarissa asked. "Where is everyone?"

Mary turned the lights back on, exposing the table filled with cake and presents and the 'Happy Birthday' banner hanging overhead.

"Happy Birthday!" everyone yelled.

Clarissa looked at Mary and then Bradley. Her happy face crumbled into tears and she rushed to her father's arms. Bradley bent down and gathered her close. "Are you okay?" he asked tenderly.

She nodded and sniffed. "I'm just too happy," she said. "And it's coming out in tears."

Bradley hugged her tighter and nodded, looking up at Mary. "I know just how you feel."

Chapter Fifty-eight

It took Clarissa only one try to blow out the candles, and Mary would never tell that she had Mike by her side assisting in her efforts. All the Brennan boys were duly impressed with her lung capacity.

She loved the dollhouse and all of the tiny furniture and accessories that went with it. Lucky claimed the second floor bedroom as her own and spent most of the party knocking things out of the house and onto the floor.

The other gifts were opened in record time, and appropriate hugs and thank yous were offered. Clarissa was nearly overwhelmed. "I've never had a party like this in my whole life," she said as she pushed another piece of chocolate cake into her mouth.

Mary waited until the noise had died down and the cake had been eaten. Then she brought out the box with the quilt.

"Another gift?" Clarissa asked.

"A special gift," Mary explained. "And there is a little love in this gift from all of us. But mostly, it's a gift from your mommy Jeannine."

Joyce wiped a tear from her eye, and Bill placed his arm around his wife and pulled her close.

"But, mommy Jeannine is in heaven," Clarissa said. "How could she send me a gift?"

Mary placed the box in Clarissa's lap. "Why don't you open it?" she said. "And then I'll tell you about it."

Clarissa almost reverently took the wrapping paper off the box and then carefully lifted the top. "Oh, it's beautiful," she said, lifting the quilt up. "And it has all my favorite colors."

Mary shook her head. She hadn't even noticed that the quilt did indeed have all of the colors Clarissa loved best.

"When you were a tiny baby, just like Mikey is now," Mary said. "Your mommy Jeannine bought all of the material to make this quilt for you. She must have known you pretty well already, because she picked out all of your favorite colors. Then she cut up the fabric into squares to make you this quilt."

Mary paused as her heart filled with sorrow for the mother who couldn't be there with her daughter. "Even though she couldn't be here with you," Mary said, her voice filled with emotion. "She wanted you to have this quilt from her. She wanted you to know how much she loves you."

"She still loves me?" Clarissa asked.

"Oh yes, darling," Joyce said. "I know your mommy Jeannine still loves you. Just as much as your mommy Mary does."

Mary took a deep breath and smiled at Joyce. "Thank you," she said.

Joyce shook her head. "No, thank you."

Then Mary turned back to Clarissa. "So, all of the people who love you helped finish the quilt," Mary explained. "Your daddy, your grandpas and your uncles took all of you to the park so we could keep it a surprise."

"And your Auntie Katie brought over her quilting frame and we set it up and everyone quilted it," Mary continued. She pointed to the tiny stitches in the material. "Each little stitch is a little bit of love. Can you count how many stitches are on the quilt?"

Clarissa shook her head. "There are too many."

Mary smiled and kissed her daughter. "Exactly. And that's how much we love you," she said. "Too much to count."

Bradley knelt down next to Clarissa on the other side. "So, even though your mommy Jeannine started this quilt out of love, she let all of us put our love into it, too," he explained.

Clarissa hugged the quilt to herself. "I will keep this always and always and always."

Chapter Fifty-nine

The house was finally quiet as Mary made her way to say goodnight to Clarissa. She opened the door to find the new quilt securely tucked into Clarissa's arms. Clarissa looked up from her pillow. "I had a great day," she said, yawning widely.

Mary sat next to her on the bed. "You had a busy day," she said. "And a great day."

"I love my new grandma and grandpa."

"And they love you, too," Mary replied, stroking Clarissa's head. "It really meant a lot to them when you invited them to come back and visit soon. That was sweet."

Clarissa shrugged. "I want them to come," she said.

"Me, too," Mary replied.

"Are you tired?" Clarissa asked.

Mary nodded. "Yes, I've had a busy day, too."

Clarissa sat up in bed, placed her hand on Mary's belly and felt it move. She giggled. "I don't think Mikey's tired," she said.

Smiling, Mary shook her head. "No, I think Mikey is ready to dance the night away," she replied.

Clarissa giggled. Then she stopped and studied Mary for a moment.

"What?" Mary asked, feeling a little pleased that she was starting to get mom powers.

"I think I saw something today," she said.

"What?" Mary asked, concerned.

"I think I saw mommy Jeannine," she said. "Just for a minute when I opened my quilt."

Mary hugged Clarissa. "I would not be surprised," she said. "I saw her today, too, when we were all making the quilt. I think the quilt was important to her."

Clarissa brought the quilt to her cheek. "I will always love it," she said.

"And your mommy Jeannine will always love you," Mary said, placing a kiss on the top of Clarissa's head. "Just like I will always love you."

Clarissa snuggled back down into her bed and smiled up at Mary. "I'll always love you, too," she said.

"That's the best thing I've heard all day," Mary said. She stood up and walked over to the door. "Good night, sweetheart. Sweet dreams."

Chapter Sixty

Mary pulled her SUV into the parking spot in front of her office, surprised that it was one of the only spots left on the street. She stepped out of her vehicle and looked around. People were everywhere. "What in the world?" she questioned, pulling her coat tighter around herself and quickly grabbing her purse so she could get into her office before anyone could see her.

Black Friday was generally not a huge shopping day for downtown Freeport because of all of the deals at the big-name chain stores, which is why the Freeport Downtown Development Foundation held its Christmas Walk on the Saturday after Black Friday. That was the only reason, quite frankly, Mary had even bothered getting out of bed. She had to decorate her office windows before the Christmas Walk.

She unlocked the door and hurried inside, keeping the blinds that covered the large display windows closed for now. She slipped her coat off and looked at her reflection in the mirror. Most of her clothes were getting uncomfortably tight, so she'd borrowed a pair of Bradley's sweatpants, which were not only too big, but also too long. So, she had pulled a pair of thick, athletic socks up over the bottoms to keep them in place. She was wearing one of her father's cast-off flannel shirts that had paint stains on the front. She hadn't bothered putting on make-up, and she had just pulled her hair back in a ponytail because— "No one was supposed to be downtown," she said to her reflection. "Who didn't get the memo? Downtown is closed today."

With a frustrated sigh, she walked over to the storage closet and pulled out the large, plastic containers of Christmas decorations. As she carried the containers to her desk, she remembered Stanley coming into her store last year and chastising her because she hadn't untangled them before she put them away for storage. "Well, I'll show him," she muttered, opening the first box.

She stared inside in shock and horror. Instead of the neat little piles she'd imagined, the lights were one big ball of tangled mess. "I thought I…" then she paused and shook her head. "No. No, I guess I didn't."

Picking up the bewildering jumble of green and white, she inserted the only visible plug into the outlet and tried to carry it back to her desk. Unfortunately, the untangled cord was only about three feet long, so instead of sitting at her desk, Mary was obliged to sit on the floor with the ball of lights in her lap.

"Bah-humbug," she muttered as she tried to weave the wires in and out of each other.

She heard the bell over the door chime but couldn't get up from the tangled mess. "Stanley?" she asked. "Is that you?"

"Mary O'Reilly?" a strange male voice asked.

Crap!

"My office is closed," she called out, praying they would just leave.

"That doesn't matter to us," the voice called back in excitement.

Mary noticed that it seemed to be getting brighter in her office. She pushed the lights off her lap, creating a bigger mess, and struggled to stand up. "Please, I don't…" she said as she began to stand.

"Smile, Mary O'Reilly," the man behind the video camera yelled. "Because you're on this week's episode of Ghost Discoverers."

"Oh, hell, no!" Mary exclaimed.

# # #

About the author: Terri Reid lives near Freeport, the home of the Mary O'Reilly Mystery Series, and loves a good ghost story. An independent author, Reid uploaded her first book "Loose Ends – A Mary O'Reilly Paranormal Mystery" in August 2010. By the end of 2013, "Loose Ends" had sold over 200,000 copies. She has sixteen other books in the Mary O'Reilly Series, the first books in the following series - "The Blackwood Files," "The Order of Brigid's Cross," and "The Legend of the Horsemen." She also has a stand-alone romance, "Bearly in Love." Reid has enjoyed Top Rated and Hot New Release status in the Women Sleuths and Paranormal Romance category through Amazon US. Her books have been translated into Spanish, Portuguese and German and are also now also available in print and audio versions. Reid has been quoted in a number of books about the self-publishing industry including "Let's Get Digital" by David Gaughran and "Interviews with Indie Authors: Top Tips from Successful Self-Published Authors" by Claire and Tim Ridgway. She was also honored to have some of her works included in A. J. Abbiati's book "The NORTAV Method for Writers – The Secrets to Constructing Prose Like the Pros."

She loves hearing from her readers at author@terrireid.com

Other Books by Terri Reid:

Mary O'Reilly Paranormal Mystery Series:

Mary O'Reilly Short Stories

The Order of Brigid's Cross (Sean's Story)

The Blackwood Files (Art's Story)

File One: Family Secrets

PRCD Case Files: The Ghosts Of New Orleans -A Paranormal Research and Containment Division Case File

Eochaidh: Legend of the Horseman (Book One)

Bearly in Love

CPSIA information can be obtained
at www.ICGtesting.com
Printed in the USA
LVHW082157051118
596081LV00018B/324/P